Breath, Go Away and Other Stories

Sriman Narayanan works for a leading credit-card-issuing company in a senior leadership position in credit risk management. He has primarily worked in the financial services industry throughout his long career—at HSBC (USA), GE Capital (India) and Standard Chartered Bank (India).

He writes about anything that tugs at his heart, mostly about life, love and relationships. His writings have a philosophical tinge.

He lives at Bentonville, Arkansas with his wife and son.

You can write to him at srimanpj@gmail.com to get to know him better, or to share your thoughts on this book.

Breath, Go Away

and Other Stories

SRIMAN NARAYANAN

RUPA

Published by
Rupa Publications India Pvt. Ltd 2015
7/16, Ansari Road, Daryaganj
New Delhi 110002

Sales Centres:
Allahabad Bengaluru Chennai
Hyderabad Jaipur Kathmandu
Kolkata Mumbai

ISBN: 978-81-291-3798-2

First impression 2015

10 9 8 7 6 5 4 3 2 1

Printed at HT Media Ltd., Noida

Jai Gurudev

Kṛṣṇaṁ vande jagadgurum

This book would not have been possible but for his grace, and the bundle of miracles that occurred, perhaps making it a brief story to tell at a later time!

Contents

Breath, Go Away

Rita Noel wrote to me unexpectedly. It was three years since I had left Delhi. She was a trendy and glamorous girl. She was not the kind of girl I would want to marry, I told myself. I was very sure about it.

We were just acquaintances, working in the same company, but in different teams and seated across adjacent cubes. When I left Delhi for another job in the US, she asked me for my email id, and I asked if we could take a photograph together.

I had never expected an email from her.

She wrote, 'I'm Rita. Do you remember me? We used to work together.'

I was very surprised to hear from her, and amused at what she wrote. Of course, I remembered her. I used to address her as pretty woman. She would occasionally ask me to accompany her outside the office building for her smoke breaks, with her smoking, and me drinking tea.

I replied to her, and she wrote back, 'You don't know how nice it is to receive your mails. I thought I had completely lost you. I'm glad I found your email address in some corner! My brother is in NJ. My parents are doing fine. They are desperately looking for a guy for me to get married to. It's nice to know that you are doing well there! Keep working hard and I will always pray for your success. But hey! Don't forget your friend. Keep in touch. Just in case you forgot my face, I thought of sending you some pictures.

'Take care and God Bless.'

I told her she looked stunning and as pretty as ever and said, 'I was thinking to myself, perhaps, you are the most glamorous friend that I have had :) And so with these charms and cool pictures, I think, I should ask not who has fallen for you, but whom have you fallen for? :)'

She revealed that she was being pressurized to get married to a boy of her parents' choice. She had therefore found a job in Singapore to stay away from them.

Her mail echoed a sense of despair. My heart wrenched at her plight, as my wounds were still raw and fresh. I wrote to her, offering words of strength. I was speaking from my own experience and mistakes. Thus, began our conversations, and our friendship.

She was very different from what I had originally thought of her. Beyond her glamour, I discovered that she had a very caring and sensitive side. She talked about living a life of good values and helping others. All this made her very attractive.

Three months passed. Our conversations drifted to the idea of marriage between us. At this point, I told her about my marriage that had happened a year ago, a culmination of my parents' incessant pressure. It had lasted less than three months and I had had it annulled.

She was expectedly shocked. But she was very gracious, as she told me, 'I understand what you have gone through. I still think you are a wonderful person, but I don't think my family will accept this. Anyway, I still want to be in touch with you as just a friend, and take life as it comes.'

Therefore, we planned to continue to talk just as friends. That is exactly what we did. We were in love.

Rita would constantly ask me where I had been, all the time, and why I had not come into her life earlier. She would tease me that she found me, and complain that I was such a fool to have not realized that she was always interested in me, ever since we had met in Delhi.

She recounted our very first interaction that I had forgotten until she reminded me of it. I was part of collections risk strategy analytics and we were a team of eight people, seated amidst the collections call centre floor. It was always very noisy. I was in a telephonic meeting along with my other teammate Manjeet, with my boss Sharmila in the US. We had turned on the speakerphone and were making the call from my cubicle. As we were straining to hear my boss amidst the loud din on the floor, I increased the speaker volume, and started talking loudly too.

Midway through the call, I heard a voice, 'Excuse me' above my head from the other side of my cubicle coming across the small partition wall. I stood up from my chair and looked up for a better view in the direction of the voice. It was Rita, and I gave her a blank look as to why in the world would she disturb us when we were in the middle of a serious conversation. She had a stern look, and said, 'Can you please keep your voices lower? My team is finding it difficult to make calls.'

Then I realized how loud I had been and felt apologetic. Moreover, she recalled that I didn't say a word, just gave her a 'wide sheepish smile', and went about cranking down the volume before getting back to the meeting. She said she was initially hesitant to tell me, fearing I may get offended, as I was senior in rank. I was an assistant manager, and she was a team leader. Her annoyance immediately evaporated on looking at my sheepish smile and friendly reaction. It was interesting to hear her perspective on that little incident and that it had made a significant first impression on her mind.

One day, she told me, 'My friend asked me what you do. I told her that you smile a lot, because you have the most innocent smile in the entire world!'

As I smiled, she continued, 'You really can take away anybody's anger with your sheepish smile! If I was very mad at you and you smiled at me the way you do, I would forget all my anger. I mean it.'

After a thoughtful pause, she added, 'In fact, you are the

kind of guy who could never be someone else, even if you made a deliberate effort to fake it. You can't because you are genuine and unique, and that is what makes you different.'

She would frequently say, 'I have been thinking of you perpetually. You really are on my mind all the time.'

She talked in such an adorable manner and said such cute things, in a manner that no woman had said to me before.

In our phone conversations, I had told her a few times that I wanted to give chaste kisses to my pretty woman.

She had responded amidst giggles, 'Slap Venumma?'[1] Her Tamil accent was very adorable. She had picked up a few lines in Tamil from her friends in Singapore.

We decided to meet when I visited Bangalore the following month.

As planned, a month later, I left for India and reached Bangalore. She reached there the next morning. She had booked a late evening flight to Dehra Dun for the same day, as she planned to visit her parents there and tell them about us. We planned to marry, whether or not her parents agreed.

I went to the airport to meet her. I was going to be seeing her in person after more than four years. I was a little nervous.

When she saw me, she shot a volley of questions at me, 'Do you feel the fluttering of my senses? Do you feel the radiance on my face when you say something cute? Do you know I think of you almost all the time? Do you know I have

---

[1]Do you want a slap.

already started dreaming of us together with my eyes open?'

I felt truly blessed. Isn't it a divine blessing to have the love of a woman that you love? I was overwhelmed with gratitude and muttered a silent prayer.

We drove to the airport, later that night. She was in tears. She did not want to leave me and go.

'I want to get married to you. I want to have kids with you. I can't seem to wait any longer. I have told you always that I don't care if my parents approve of our marriage or not. You are mine,' she said, amidst her sobs. I was misty eyed.

Two days later, after she had reached Dehra Dun, my world began to crumble. She told me her parents were forcing her into an engagement with a guy and resigned to fate, she might as well give in. I was shaken and speechless. Nothing she said made any sense.

I asked her, 'How can you even talk like this, after everything?'

She replied, 'Tell me, what do I tell my parents? That you were married before, and your marriage was annulled. This won't work. Don't wait for me. My parents won't understand this.'

I was devastated. I was not even sure if I would survive. I still hoped against hope that she was merely saying all that exasperated by her parents' pressure and didn't mean what she said.

Four months passed. I don't know how I survived those months. One day, I broke down and wept aloud on the phone. I could not control myself any longer. She was shaken that

I was crying and said we should talk later. That was the last time I heard her voice. A month later was my birthday. She didn't call me.

I typed out a note to her. That was the last time I wrote to her.

Breath, Go Away

I'm not hurt that you walked away,
Leaving me behind,
Not caring to look back to see how I fare.
Baby, I'm not hurt that you left me,
Going silent to my mail, and call,
Not writing or talking to me.

You walked into my life,
When I had not known you,
Telling me a dream that I had not seen,
Pulling me away from my life into yours,
And when I'm in your dream, you knock me down,
With a violence that I haven't known,
And leave me forever, to promise a dream to another one?

What becomes of me, now?
When heart is consumed by fire, mind is lifeless,
The spirit that soared once is paralysed, and life seems useless,
Shall I pray, that my breath, leave me too, as you have?

Baby, I am not hurt that you don't love me,
But I am hurt that you made me think that you love me,
By telling me,
That you love me.

The year is 2006. A year and four months have passed. You ask me now, if I really meant what I wrote. No, as I had unequal parts of pain, hurt and anger then.

Now, I look at the entire episode differently. Maybe, she had a story of her own, her own compulsions, and her own reasons for what she did. Perhaps, we were never meant to be. Maybe, she was destined to be with someone much better than I was. Possibly, I didn't deserve her. Or perhaps, it was the play of destiny. Sometimes, there are certain things in life that will remain a permanent mystery. This is one such.

I don't think of her much now. The few times that I feel the pain, I breathe it away and whisper, 'Breath, Go Away', inhaling deeply, embracing the fresh breath of air, muttering a heartfelt thanks to God for giving me the strength to move on and be able to get over her.

Time is the best ally for a broken heart.

It is 2010. I'm married and I have a very loving and beautiful wife. Looking back, I make more sense out of all my life events. Whatever happens is for the very best.

Time is the best ally for everything.

Kisses to God

It was early in the morning. My phone rang. I looked at the name that flashed, and said in a tone of surprise, 'Hi Poonam.'

'Shyam, hasn't it been a year since you moved out of Mumbai? I'm coming to Bangalore tomorrow for business and returning on Saturday noon. I was hoping we could meet for coffee in the morning before I head to the airport,' she said.

'Look forward to seeing you. So meet you at the Barista at MG Road at 10?' I asked.

'Ok, I'm on my way to work. See you on Saturday! There is lot to catch up on!' she said.

Poonam and I had worked for the same company in Mumbai before I changed job, and relocated to Bangalore.

She is very pretty looking and a kind-hearted girl. When I joined the team, her kindness touched me when she volunteered to drive me around the city for sightseeing in her car, on a weekend. My friends have often suggested that a beautiful face and a beautiful heart rarely coexist. It is always one or the other. But in her, I found both.

She had a curious mind. She had peppered me that entire day with varied questions about my family, general interests, career aspirations and my view on life.

She had asked me such offbeat questions as, 'What has been your biggest regret in life?'

I had smiled and replied, 'I have a long list. One, I cannot sing. Two, I cannot dance and three, I cannot play any musical instrument!'

She had laughed loudly and said, 'You are funny!'

I had enjoyed my conversations with her, chatting away, which was very unusual for me. She was a good listener and I felt calm talking to her. My friends commended me for being a good listener, but I truly had no inkling what that meant to them, until I had my own experience of being listened to.

We had exchanged a few emails when I left Mumbai, but we had not been in touch for almost a year. Hence, I was surprised to receive her call that morning, and felt good at the prospect of seeing her, after a long time.

It was a warm day and I thanked the weather. We decided to sit outside the coffee shop, overlooking the road. She ordered a latte, and I asked for a mocha. She talked about her work, her parents, and the shopping she had done last evening.

Midway, she paused abruptly and asked in a soft voice, 'Shyam, I noticed the sombre tone in your voice on the phone. I see it on your face too. You look and sound perturbed. Is everything ok? Are you happy with your new job?'

I was taken aback at the question. I rested my coffee on the table and asked slowly, 'How do you read so well?'

'What is worrying you?' she persisted.

'My best friend is going through a very painful patch in his life. He is under tremendous pressure from his parents to marry, but he cannot find a girl that he really likes. I care for him a lot and I'm troubled that I don't see any solution to his misery,' I said.

Her eyes widened with deep curiosity, and she asked, 'Who is this friend? Tell me everything about him.'

I hesitated, but her kind eyes and soothing voice implored me to open up and talk. And I did.

'My friend is smart, intelligent, good looking, unassuming, and a sensitive person with a noticeable smile about him, as others often describe him,' I said.

The waiter placed the latte and mocha on the table, and said, 'Enjoy your beverage!'

As he left, I resumed, 'He had his share of attractions, infatuations, and love. The most beautiful, charming, and very smart girls were attracted to him at varying points of his life, at his school, college, and work. He is aware that he is no handsome hunk with drop-dead looks, but very much a regular guy next door. Moreover, all the attention or professions of love that he received had happened only after the women got to know him well. It was never at first sight. He is the kind of a guy who grows upon women.'

Poonam interrupted, 'I bet your friend is a good listener. Women find that to be very attractive in a man.'

I nodded my head.

'Go on,' she urged.

I continued, 'With repeated instances of women's attention and love directed at him, somewhere in his subconscious mind, he felt this was permanent. He had been naïve in thinking he would continue to meet such wonderful women in life, and so had constantly resisted reciprocating feelings of attraction and love for them that sprouted in his heart, believing love matters could wait and be pursued later. Professional career was more important and he could not afford to get distracted.'

Poonam's phone rang. She grabbed it, put it on silent mode, and said, 'Sorry.'

She quickly added, 'Your friend is a very interesting character. What's his name?'

I merely smiled and continued quietly, 'As years passed by, all Maddy's dear friends got married. His parents decided that it was high time he got married too. He was initially reluctant but gave in, and agreed to their search for a girl.

However, he was in for a big shock. Most girls that he met were not even a tad good looking compared to his beautiful friends of the past. He now bemoans that he had such wrong notions that love could wait and pursuit of career was far more important.'

Poonam stopped sipping her coffee, and rested it on the table. She pulled the chair and drew closer to me. Her eyes turned wide, and breathing deeply, she urged me to continue, and not pause.

I said, 'Finally, after a long, exhaustive, and tiresome search, on the various online matrimonial sites, he did come across one or two women that he really liked. He exchanged pictures with them and the mutual interest sustained. He met them. But, this time it was the turn of those women not to like him. The reasons could be any, and are unknown to him. Although he is very disappointed, he accepts and understands it, for he too didn't like every other person that he had met.'

I took a sip of the mocha, and continued, 'He is heart-broken and disheartened with the entire process of searching for a girl. He finds it very painful and discouraging. He weeps that every time God had sent someone beautiful in his life, he had let her go.

'He is now ready for love. He wants to fall head-over-heels in love with a girl. But love just happens unawares. You cannot wish it to happen at your whim. He feels everything is lost. All that remains in him is tears in his eyes, pain in the heart and memories of the past.

'Not smart, not good looking, not sensitive is how Maddy describes himself, now. And yes, there is still that noticeable smile. But there is something noticeable about it now. It is that the smile has faded,' I said.

Poonam stared at me, looking into my eyes silently for several seconds. A tear trickled down her cheek and she said, 'I have fallen in love with your friend.'

I was startled at her words. My mouth dropped at what she had just said.

Tears continuing to fall, she shot a question at me softly, 'Why aren't you hugging me, and kissing me yet, dammit?'

I was confounded. My head was spinning at what she had uttered.

'Are you again going to make the mistake of letting go someone beautiful that comes in your life, Maddy?' she asked, and added, 'Shyam, I know that Maddy is you.'

A tear trickled down my cheek.

I hugged her and muttered, 'Kisses to God.'

Can Men Water Plants?

When my mother was in the US, we had invited Shiela and Anand for lunch. When they came over, they brought a gift for us. It was a book. Shiela told me that she had actually wanted to gift me a potted plant, but had decided against it.

With a puzzled expression, I asked her the reason for her change of mind. She replied, 'Men can't water plants. They can't take care of them. And since you are single, and your mother is here only for a month, I decided to get you something else.'

Anand shot back with a tone of irritation, 'Shiela, you cannot make a judgment and generalize things. How can you think that all men cannot water plants? You just made that sweeping statement. Also, what do you know about him?'

Encouraged by Anand's chiding, I joined in. I said, 'Yeah, I would have surely watered it. Maybe I am not the kind who will seek out and buy a plant. But if I am given one, I would water it for sure.'

I continued to boast, 'In fact, I will never understand a man who cannot water plants and take good care of them.'

This happened six months ago. I had never imagined then that my vain boast would come to haunt me later.

Just two days ago, Swapna, who lives in the same apartment community, e-mailed that Srinath and she were going out to India for a month. She asked if I would mind taking care of their potted plants while they were away. Swapna is Sheila's sister-in-law.

I had the sneaking suspicion that Shiela must have told Swapna how I had boasted to her.

'I'm being put on a test now. OMG! Why did I have to invite this trouble? Why did I get carried away and utter such mindless words?' I bemoaned.

After a few minutes of cursing myself, I decided that I should not be so hard on myself. Come on, who else will pity me, if I don't pity myself? So what, if I had boasted? Why do they have to take it literally and hold it against me? Why this below the belt blow?

Isn't this a time to employ forgiveness and ignore what I had said? After all, I am their friend, and a very good friend at that.

My grandmother's words came hurtling into my mind. She would say, 'Today's people are so very different from my times. They have become very ruthless and have no sense of compassion.' Look at her words of wisdom; she was so right. One little innocuous statement I made, and look how they have ganged up against me on that.

I called up Praveen Purohit. He is the one that I talk to, about all trivial or important matters. And this was a very important matter.

When I finished lamenting, he said, 'Exercise your sense of logic. It may not be that Shiela and Swapna are ganging up against you. This could very well be God's doing. He must have been miffed at your vain boast.'

I countered in a puzzled tone, 'Praveen, give me a break. When did God start getting into all these little things. I doubt if he has the time or would even be concerned about it. Unlike many people, I am very regular in visiting temples; I visit once every six months. Who even does that, these days? Contrary to what you said, shouldn't God be extra compassionate to me for my sincerity, devotion, and regular visits? It was, in any case, just a vain boast that I made in a weak moment. I was carried away. Now, what is so sinful about it?' I implored.

He asked, 'Whatever it is, why are you fretting so much about watering the plants?'

He quickly added with deep concern, 'Do you have to water them in the morning, afternoon, evening, and night every day?'

I despaired, 'Close enough. I have to water them twice a week in the morning.'

After a slight pause, Praveen recovered himself and said politely, 'I had imagined far worse. This should be very easy. You can do it.'

'I'm just 29. Don't you think it is such a big responsibility to be thrust on such young shoulders? What do I know about plants? And watering them it twice a week for a month! My head is spinning just thinking of it. As such, I don't have anyone to take care of me. How will I take care of some plants,' I screamed.

Listening to our intense conversation, Praveen's wife joined in.

'Don't worry. I'm sure you will do a great job,' she said.

'There are too many complications here, Pramila!' I wailed.

'What is the complication?' she asked.

'I will tell you, just now,' I cleared my throat and started to speak, 'If I fail in taking good care of the plants, they will die. I'm not concerned about the plants dying. What I'm worried is that the word will go around. And people around me would start judging me. They would say—The guy's profile is very good. He works in a good company. He has good looks. But what is the point? He could not even take care of a few plants; leave alone taking care of a girl. What parents would want to trust him and give him the hand of their daughter?'

Controlling my tears, I asked, 'Do you see now, where I am coming from? This is so unjust. What will happen to me? How will I get married?'

Both Praveen and Pramila were choked with emotion, and they wailed in unison. 'Poor you, what will you do now?'

Hearing them cry, I cried louder and said, 'Arrey, be strong. Be strong like me. Don't cry. I will manage.'

A two-second pause later, I started to cry hard, 'I don't know how I will manage.'

Now, all three of us were crying on the phone.

In that instant, I heard a loud sound in the background on the phone. There was a sound of glass falling onto the ground and I could hear an elderly woman's voice scream with fear, '*Hey Bhagwan*!'

Later, I learnt that it was Pramila's mother, who was visiting her from India. Seeing Praveen and her daughter cry on the phone, she was shaken and had a panic attack and swooned. Her husband had been keeping very ill in India since a week and she had imagined the worst.

Seeing the complete empathy and emotional connection, I realized that they were my 'soul mates'. I understood now, what that feeling of having a soul mate is. Years ago, I had talked to a girl in Canada, who had told me that one could have many soul mates in life aside from the spouse. I was shocked to hear it.

I had asked her, 'Isn't that a sacrilege? In a happy marriage, how can there be a soul mate aside from your spouse?'

She explained to me at length about the concept of soul mates.

I felt that I could not share all my sorrows with just

one set of soul mates. After all, that is why there is more than one soul mate, I told myself. So I decided to share my grief with my other soul mates. My other soul mates? Who were they? I didn't know. It was for me to discover now.

I thought hard and after several hours of mental labour, I had a feeble feeling that my cousin, Anupama Sowmya must be my other soul mate. I needed to talk to her. She was seven months pregnant then and she used to sleep early. So I decided to call her right then before it got late. I called her and narrated the entire episode.

She asked with a touch of irritation, 'What is the problem here? Assume the worst, the plants die, and the word goes around. So what? Why do you rely on them to find a girl? You find your girl, dude.'

'What are you saying? Didn't I tell you what the Tarot card reader told me,' I asked in anguish.

'No,' she said in a cold tone.

'When I was in Bangalore, I had met a very renowned woman, who could read a person's future from the tarot cards. That was a few days after I met Vandana Jain. I asked the woman what the cards foretold on the prospects of marriage between Vandana and me. You know what she said? "This match is good for Vandana, but not for you."

'I asked her why. She said, "Vandana has a very strong temperament and always has anger on the edge. You are not capable of handling such furious tempers." I was zapped at the uncanny precision of her voicing my exact thoughts and apprehensions about Vandana.'

'What is your point? I don't see any relevance,' Anupama interrupted.

I asked her to be patient, and elaborated, 'The point is that she is so accurate in her reading. I asked her this question: "How will I find my girl? Please excuse me asking such a pointed question. I have put my profile on a few matrimonial sites. And nothing has happened. If you guide me as to how I will meet her, I will focus my efforts accordingly. Will it be from shaadi.com or jeevansaathi.com? Right now, I am spending equal time on both. Which one, should I spend more time on?"

'She said, "Boy, you will not find your own girl. It will not happen from any of the matrimonial sites, where you are currently searching. Your girl will be found through a friend of yours. One of your friends will be your matchmaker. It is only a friend of yours, who will bring your light of life to you."'

I continued in a distressed tone, 'Now do you see the evil play of fate? If I'm destined to meet my girl through my friends, and when the plants die and the word goes around, you know how all my friends are connected with each. Then, what will become of me? No one is going to give a good reference of me.

'I'm doomed,' I said and began to sob.

I heard a loud wail from Anupama. It was louder than my sobs.

She said, 'Poor you, what will become of you now?'

My heart twisted with pain and I told her, 'Listen, you

are a strong woman. You are a mother to be. Please don't cry. I am a strong person too. I will manage.'

After a minute, I said, 'I don't know how I will manage, Anupama.'

I started to cry too and we both continued our wails.

After a while, I got tired of crying and so I stopped. However, she continued to cry and a pang of guilt struck me. So I resumed my crying.

That night, her husband Sharath was so mad at me because I had made her go through such stress despite her pregnancy that he instructed Anupama not to ever talk to me or take my calls. I was horrified by his callous indifference to my plight. I could only remember my grandmother's words.

I felt alone. I could not talk to her anymore. I had lost a soul mate. I went to my closet and pulled out a few old diaries to look up long forgotten names. Maybe, I would find my other soul mates there.

After flipping through a few pages, I came across Hema Verma's name. She was my next-door neighbour in India. She must be my other soul mate. I murmured that she was my soul mate number 4. Then I had a doubt. Or was she soul mate number 3? Should I still count Anupama as my soul mate or not?

As I was debating, just then, Ramya called. Then it struck me that my sister was yet another soul mate.

No sooner did she ask, 'How are you?', than I replied,

'Akka,[2] how did you know I was in such distress? You are so perceptive.'

I started telling her my tale of woes. What will become of me? Why did I boast in vain?

The saga continued, and in the process, I discovered my many 'soul mates'!

(Although this is a fictional account, it is based on some true life incidents. I was indeed given three potted plants to take care of, for ten days. I did meet a girl, who initiated me into the concept of soul mates. And I did meet the Tarot Card reader at Bangalore, although her prediction of how I would meet my girl was off, while she was correct about the timing of my marriage!)

---

[2]Sister in Tamil and Telugu.

A Shiver of Joy

I was set to travel to San Jose to attend a get together event organized by the NBIF—Network of Bay Area Indian Families. It was a weekend event, filled with lots of Bollywood music, Indian food, outdoor activities like hiking, scavenger hunt, sports and a cultural segment, where participants were encouraged to showcase their talents, be it in dance, music, instruments or just about anything, to entertain the audience.

I planned to share one of my pieces of writing in the cultural segment. Writing is my passion, and I write about anything that touches me deeply. The event was set to attract about hundred families.

I wanted to get some feedback on the piece of writing I had in mind, before sharing it in front of the large crowd at the event. So I sent it to Deepika, my cousin, to a friend who is an avid reader, and to Ramya Rohini, my sister. My writing was in two parts, and I just sent the first part to all of them and added a line in the end, 'to be continued...'

The next day morning, there was a flurry of emails in my inbox, from each of them.

Deepika wrote, 'What is wrong with you? Please don't send such kind of writing to my office mail id.'

'My friend wrote, 'Mmmmmmmm...I'm intrigued. Send me the second part soon.'

My sister, who is older to me by three years, wrote, 'Thamba,[3] I think we should get you married sooooon. I will call you tomorrow night...'

On Saturday morning, I took the flight to San Jose, and I carried a printed copy of my writing with me. The cultural segment was scheduled that evening at 6 p.m., followed by dinner at 8 p.m. I was brimming with excitement, and I was greatly looking forward to it. It started sharp at six. There were many young adults in their teens and twenties, fathers and mothers and elderly people who were sixty plus, who displayed various talents, mostly centred around singing and playing instruments; and there were a few solo dances too.

When my turn came, I briefly introduced myself and said, 'I work for a financial services firm in risk function. So risk management is my profession, but writing is my passion.'

I continued, 'What I have today, is a piece that I wrote

---

[3]Brother in Telugu.

in a moment of deep ecstasy. It is in two parts.'

'It is titled—'A Shiver of Joy', I said and pulled out the pages stuffed inside my trouser pocket.

I started to read, the same piece that I had sent to Deepika, my friend, and to my sister.

'Shiver of Joy—Part 1,' I said and continued, 'A shiver of joy ran through me. A thin smile slowly trickled in. The lips widened as the trickle raced across my face at feverish pace and hit the eyes, as it reached the ears. And I closed my eyes for a moment with a silent sense of elation. It was the first time ever. A deep quiet ecstasy was silently whirling inside and I let the feeling linger for I wanted to savour every bit of it.'

I paused, and looked around the hall. I could sense an uneasy silence and see everyone looking horror-struck. Some of them, particularly the elders in the crowd, were giving me hostile and disapproving looks.

Unperturbed, I continued to read with a wide smile on my face, 'Shiver of Joy—Part 2'.

'Next, I slowly lifted my hand. With both, nervous excitement and a little fright, I wanted to feel. I wanted to touch. I wanted to know if it was as it seemed to be. Yes, it was. Felt perfect. At last, I did get it perfect, after so many times of toil.

'Proud I was! Soft, delicate, fluffy and chubby. A real delight! One, two, three...and so I counted those small tiny angels smiling at me. There were twelve of them. I am yet to call and tell everyone that I made these idlis all on my own. Why so much elation? Yes, indeed! For these are from batter that I made from the start, from the very scratch, step by step, all by myself.

'I was relishing the ability to create something so beautiful. The ease of the power to create something so good that would gratify the tongue immensely. It has been, for long, deprived of any delicacy, and just left to the mercy of the cooking skills of its master. But this tiny success seems to be a fresh breather, holding promise for the future.

'Maybe the power above, not willing to hear anymore the loud wails and moans of the tongue, finally decided to show a shred of compassion towards it, and blessed its master with a little skill and graced him with the ability to make at least one dish perfectly! Yeah! Even the higher power seems to be bound by the law of averages, as it could not let the master continue tormenting his tongue forever! Hail the law of averages!'

I looked at the crowd, and with a wide grin asked, 'But the idlis aside, what did you all really think it was?'

The whole crowd burst into a roar of laughter and clapped.

'Mission accomplished,' I thought. I had wanted to indulge in a play of words, and mislead the audience into wild imagination and entertain them with an unexpected twist.

Yes, it had the same effect on my cousin, friend, and my sister, when I shared with them the second part the next day.

Deepika wrote, 'Oh my god...as I was reading this, I

was laughing so hard that I had tears in my eyes! I haven't had such a hearty laugh in a long time…'

My friend wrote, 'I was very curious to know what you were referring to in the beginning and started to laugh so badly when I realized it was nothing other than an idli.'

My sister wrote, 'Huh! You send such freaky writing...I had to chant the hanuman chalisa a whopping 108 times to rub off the wicked imagination...'

Priceless Conversations

Have you ever had a conversation, short or long, and felt it was an absolute joy and delight and wished to indulge in more? It is a conversation, which is engaging, absorbing, amusing, interesting and spontaneous!

'Priceless,' I would say, when asked to describe the whole feeling.

Most Sunday mornings, I go to my friends' house for group meditation. About ten to fifteen people, who are members of the same meditation group, turn up and we sit together to meditate for an hour and disperse. My friends have two small kids, and I am fond of the younger one, Gopika. She is three, and is extremely adorable when she talks, for she gets very animated in her expressions. A poem I enjoy reciting to her is:

'Roses are red, violets are blue,
Sugar is white, honey is sweet,
And so are you'.

Moreover, she bursts into peals of laughter, as she hears the last line. I become amused that this little child is also capable of seeing the poetic association.

A year later, I travelled to Phoenix for a gathering of members all across the country, hosted by our meditation group. Gopika was also around. I repeated this poem to her and she lit up with her usual smile. Her older cousin Malavika, eight-years-old, who was standing beside her, turned around, looked at me, and said, 'This is weirddddd.'

I was taken aback, but managed to smile, and wondered if my poem was cheesy.

I asked her, 'Why is it weird?'

'Because, it is weirddd,' she replied.

I was stumped at her response. I overcame my shock and smiled as I realized my mistake. I should have been careful, and looked around before reciting the poem to Gopika, as Malavika must have felt left out from the attention when she overheard me.

I met Malavika again at another such event, five months later. She was restless and sleepy. I said a hello to her mom and remarked that Malavika was the smartest kid that I had ever met. That very moment, Malavika's one eye opened up wide, she gave me a half wink and a wide smile. I laughed aloud at her snap reaction to my compliment even in her sleepy state.

To make up for my mistake the last time, I took her aside, and recited the same poem to her, hoping she would be pleased now that I was directing it to her.

I took her hand, looked into her eyes and with a smile, I said,

'Roses are red, violets are blue,
Sugar is white, honey is sweet,
And so are you!'

'This is horrible,' she said.

I became speechless. After all, the poem is indeed cheesy, I thought. I felt a huge sense of shame.

'Why is this horrible?' I pleaded.

She replied,

'Because, I don't like sweets,
I don't like flowers,
I don't like poetry.'

'What do you like then?' I enquired, with a tiny smile.

'I like toys,
I like makeup,
I like gifts,' she replied.

'So you don't like sweets?'

'No! Chocolates, and only sometimes,' she said.

I smiled.

'You don't like sweets, but you like to apply makeup and admire yourself in the mirror to see how sweet you are?' I asked, pretending to look puzzled.

She said loudly, 'You are not making any sense!'

I was getting nervous now, but managed to continue to smile, and asked,

'You say you don't like being called "sweet", right?' I asked.

'Yes,' she nodded.

'Yet you say you like makeup. And why would you do that, except to look at yourself in the mirror to see how pretty and sweet you are?' I said, laboriously illustrating my point.

'You are not getting it,' she said with a sense of despair, 'I like applying makeup on others, not on myself.'

I slapped myself mentally for making an erroneous assumption.

I smiled and asked her, 'Ok, tell me what gifts you like to get?'

She replied, 'How would I know?'

I told her, 'If you don't say, then you could end up getting gifts that you don't like.'

She beamed and said, 'Then, I would give them to others.'

I reasoned with her, 'But gifts are given for you to keep. Aren't they?'

With all the innocence in her little eyes, she wondered, 'But when I grow up, I might throw them away.'

I laughed aloud, and told her, 'That's ok as long as you keep them for a year! Now let's take a picture of this smartest little girl that I have ever met.'

Click.

It is indeed a great pleasure to have such simple and joyful conversations with little children, who exude both innocence and intelligence, defying their age.

That Something

Some things happen in life that we don't understand.

It was the year 2000. I had just changed my job and moved to Delhi from Cochin. It was the third job in my career, and a big geographical shift all the way from the south. I missed the idli, sambar and filter coffee greatly, and the Tamil movie—*Alai Payuthe* (*Saathiya* in Hindi) that was released around that time.

Something unexpected...

It happened then. Someone said 'something'. I was a little amused to hear that, for it was the first time. Next, my college-going cousin e-mailed me and said 'that something'. I was a little more amused, hearing that for the second time from yet another person. Later, a friend of mine made a mention of it in her letter. The amusement, slowly, gave way to a smile, though I still dismissed all that they said.

I went back home for a month's vacation, later that year in December. The kids of my next door neighbour, seeing me after a long time, greeted me, shouting out aloud—'that something'. And the smile gave way to a sense of little excitement. In a family gathering, a distant uncle of mine walked up to me, said 'that something' and walked past. Moreover, at home, my nephew, while watching TV, suddenly turned around, looked at me and commented 'that something'. Coming from my nephew who was just six-years-old, I was plain amazed.

All this was a strange, unexpected, intriguing experience, so to say.

Something expected...

Later, when I continued to encounter repeat episodes of a similar kind, I was more than plain amazed. And by then, I had got used to them as they became so very regular and predictable, coming from a wide cross section of people across genders and age groups.

One day at work, with nothing better to do, I had to tell Sandhya, the only co-worker of mine with a similar ethnic background from the south, of the funny and amusing things that were happening around me. I knew that she would poke fun at me, when I finished telling her the entire thing. She was extremely witty and had a great sense of humour. She always found something to laugh about in everything. She made fun of people in such a way that even her victims laughed and did not find it offensive. At least that was the case with me, and I bore the brunt of her fun machine, as I was her favourite target.

I enjoyed her wit and humour, and so, I didn't mind telling her—although, I knew that I was inviting sheer trouble for myself. And as expected, when I finished relating all the strange incidents, she burst out laughing. Though she was in partial agreement on 'that something', it was not in her nature to acknowledge it. She, instead, teasingly maintained that 'that something' so many had told me was completely untrue and cautioned me not to get carried away.

And I would try to get even with her by coming up with some witty rejoinders like how the other day, while walking on the road, I had been literally mobbed by people mistaking me for someone else and so these days, whenever I go out, I wear a sign that says in bold: 'I'm not who you think I am!' These were all products of manufactured fantasy, made up by me in an attempt to provide witty retorts to her. There were many more like that. Overall, they did make for some good time-pass discussions, fun and laughter.

One day, Sandhya invited me to her home for dinner, as her mother-in-law was visiting from Chennai, and she would like to meet me. When I went to their home, her mother-in-law was so very surprised on seeing me. She pulled Sandhya aside in a room and asked her with complete wonderment in a hushed tone, *'Evan siricha, apadiye madhavan mari ey irukan elle?'* Translated from Tamil, it is—When he smiles, doesn't he look just like Madhavan (Actor Madhavan)?

Yes, this was the same 'that something' told by many!

Many more incidents like these followed; that of more people talking about the supposed resemblance highlighted by my wide, toothy smile. I lost count of them, or so it seemed to me. It became so common that at most times there was a pattern. When I met people for the very first time, they would exclaim, 'You look so very familiar,' struggling to place me exactly and then after a few seconds, would say, 'Oh goodness, you look like Madhavan.'

Obviously, there existed many with whom I had checked, out of curiosity, if they too felt the same way about the resemblance and they said that they didn't. Therefore, they don't get a mention here!

Something unexpected...

It was the year 2003. As I walked out of a temple, there was this familiar line, 'You look so very familiar' and the accompanying pattern of a struggling attempt to place me. Only this time, the struggle was longer than usual. Being nice and sympathetic, I decided to help him out, and not let him struggle longer. So I said that perhaps he was seeing a faint resemblance to the Actor Madhavan in me. He shook his head profusely and said, 'No,' but continued to say that I looked familiar, but he was just not able to recall when and where he had met me earlier.

Only later, I was to realize that 'you look familiar' was a line used as a ruse and an ice-breaker to befriend me and get me to enrol as a member in the network marketing programme that he was associated with. Later, I got to hear more details of how they catch people off-guard in grocery stores, shopping malls, temples and give this, 'You look so familiar' ice-breaking line, warm them up, and then do a hard sell of their network marketing business with them.

Knowing this later, I felt very embarrassed at myself for the vain assumption that he was trying to place my resemblance to Madhavan, and worse, I had tried to help him out!

Three years have passed since then. Just a month ago, a sixty-five-year-old woman said it. However, such comments about the supposed resemblance have become less common now.

Some things happen in life that we don't understand. Looking at the present through the past, I don't understand why there aren't any such comments now. And looking at the past through the present, I don't either understand why there were quite so many then.

Perhaps, it was the newness of Actor Madhavan then. So anyone who remotely or vaguely resembled him, caught attention. Or perhaps the ubiquitous smile on my face has faded since then. Or perhaps it is both. But it makes for a good memory and brings a smile and laughter whenever I think of it. It is small things like these which make life a joyful experience.

Momentous Emotions

Venkat was 27 years old and working for a bank in Cochin. He moved to a new apartment complex that was also closer to his office, and had better amenities with a gym and a swimming pool. He lived in a one-bedroom apartment on the first floor, and across the hallway, was a two-bedroom apartment, where a group of three girls lived. They worked at Taj Gateway Hotel as interns.

On the day of the move, Venkat met Lisa in the hallway, and she said, 'Hi, I'm Lisa Jacob. I live across your apartment with my friends. You have made a good choice to move in here, this is a great apartment community.'

Venkat replied, 'Hi Lisa! I'm Venkat Nayak. I work at the GTB bank, which is three blocks away. I'm glad to hear this is a great place to live.'

Lisa offered him tea, and introduced her other two roommates, Sapna and Prasitha.

That was Venkat's first interaction with Lisa and he took a great liking to her. She was a tall and very attractive woman with sharp, beautiful eyes.

Over the months, Venkat, Lisa, Sapna, and Prasitha became very good friends, and they would hang out together in the evenings and weekends, playing board games, watching movies, exploring restaurants, and going on long drives. Venkat had a white Hyundai Santro car and the girls just loved to be driven around.

One day, as Venkat returned from work and took the stairwell to his apartment, he saw Lisa dressed in a pink saree, ahead of him by a few flights of stairs.

He called out to her and she turned and said, 'Hi Venkat.'

'You are looking so ravishing in this stunning pink.'

Lisa smiled, and said, 'Hey, do you want to have some tea?'

'I would love to. It has been a long day at work,' he said.

'Ok, come in ten minutes. I will have a change over, meanwhile. Sapna and Prasitha are doing a late shift, and they wouldn't be here for a while.'

After about fifteen minutes, Venkat rang the doorbell.

Lisa opened the door, and said, 'Come on in, Venkat. I have made the tea and it is simmering on the stove. Be seated, and I will get the tea for us.'

Venkat sat on the sofa, smelling the aroma of the cardamom tea. Lisa made excellent tea, and that was one of her specialities in her long list of culinary skills.

She brought a tray with two cups, offered one to Venkat, and said, 'So you are twenty-seven years old, with a plush job in a bank in a senior position. I suppose you are earning mega-bucks. You have a car. So your parents must be eager to get you married.'

'Well, I want to find my girl,' he said.

'What kind of a girl do you desire?' she asked.

'A wholesome beauty. Let's say I really don't have any preference that my girl should have long hair, or short hair, be fair skinned or dusky, from the north or the south, a Hindu or a Christian. She should be attractive to my eyes, and a good human being. That is all that I ask for in my girl,' he said.

'In fact, my idea of wholesome beauty is someone exactly like you,' he added and laughed.

'Shut up! Don't joke now,' she said, and asked, 'Haven't you found your girl yet?'

'Stop quizzing me! What about you? When do you plan to get married?' he asked.

'Very soon. My parents are looking for a guy for me. They are very sweet. They won't force me if I don't like the guy. Or if I fall in love with someone, they would support that too.'

After a pause, she said, 'Although I'm very progressive and liberal in my outlook, in matters of marriage, I have very conservative values. I consider marriage as a lifetime commitment. Whatever may happen in the marriage, the husband and wife have to work it out, and sort out the problems. Way out of marriage is not an option. So I will be very careful about the guy I marry, as I have to live my entire life with him. It is high stakes, and I will not be easily swayed by anybody I meet.'

As she finished, she smiled and asked, 'So Mr, have you found your girl yet?'

Venkat said, 'I may have. But I don't think I could tell her.'

'Why?' she asked.

At that juncture, their conversation was interrupted, as Sapna and Prasitha walked in to the apartment. The topic of discussion then shifted to the perils of doing late shifts, and after an hour, Venkat bid them good night, and retired to his apartment.

The next morning, when Venkat reached his office, Vishal Sharma, who was his manager, called him to his cabin. The manager said the Pune branch office was experiencing a very high employee turnover and one senior executive had quit just yesterday.

Vishal said, 'Venkat, the Corporate Headquarters have requested me to send you on deputation to the Pune branch for three to six months. We want a strong player there, until we fill up the vacancies and stabilize attrition. This is in recognition of your ability and strong performance. I want you to leave immediately, and if at all possible, take the evening flight and report to work there tomorrow morning.'

Venkat returned to his apartment, packed his bag, and as he headed out, took out a post-it and scribbled a small note, 'Hi Lisa, Sapna, Prasitha, this is Venkat. Something urgent has come up at my office. I'm leaving for Pune branch today and will be gone for a few months. But will be back soon. Take care, all!'

Work at Pune was very busy, and time flew. Six months passed.

One day, his cell phone rang on a late evening. He didn't recognize the number. He picked it up and said, 'Hello.'

'Venkat?' the voice at the other end asked.

'Hey Lisaaaaa, my dear! What a surprise! How did you get my number?' he asked.

'You are so very mean, Venkat. You didn't even bother to leave your phone number. Just left a short cryptic note, huh?'

'I'm sorry, Lisa. It happened very suddenly. But I'm really glad you called me. You made my day!'

'I went to your office yesterday, enquiring about you and got your number. Anyway, do you know why I called?'

He laughed and said, 'To tell me that you have fallen in love with me?'

'Shut up, Venkat! I'm getting married. He is in the Middle East. His parents are from our neighbouring village and they reached out to my parents. I have been speaking to him over the phone and emails for about three months. He is a very nice guy and I made up my mind last week. The wedding will be at the local church in Kottayam next month. It is on the 22nd, a Sunday and you should come.'

'Lisa, congratulations. This is exciting, and great news. But are you sure you want me to attend your wedding?'

'What do you mean?' she asked.

'At your wedding, when the priest utters these words, "If anyone can show just cause to why these two should not be joined together in matrimony, then let him speak now, or forever hold his peace," what if I stand up, protest the matrimony, and say that I'm deeply in love with you?' he said and laughed aloud.

'Venkat, shut up! Don't say such a freaky thing. In any case, you had your chance all this while, but you never professed it to me.'

'Do you mean if I had asked you to marry me, you would have?' he asked, taken by surprise.

'I don't know! I may have given it a serious consideration! You are a gentleman, caring, nice and soft-spoken. You are smart, intelligent, and have a sense of humour. You have good looks and are not a bad guy, after all,' she chuckled.

There were a few seconds of silence.

She asked, 'Hey, are you there?'

'Sorry, I was suddenly reminded of this wedding scene from the movie, *The Wedding Planner*. As the priest utters those very same words, the father of the bride breaks up, with tears shining in his eyes. His emotions get the better of him and he speaks up and objects. He calls his daughter aside, and apologizes for compelling her to marry someone she doesn't like. You know, the truth and the facts remained the same. Nothing changed. But the setting and the mood was different, sufficient for the father of the bride to realize his doings, and speak up. Isn't it?'

'Yes, I have watched that movie, and remember the scene,' she said.

'I have no idea if this customary rite has ever saved anyone in real life, though?' he asked.

'It is always a nerve-wracking moment! I recall that my friend's wedding a few years ago was stopped, as the bride herself objected when the question was asked, as she was in love with someone else. My friend, he was heart-broken at that time, but I think it was good for both of them in the long run,' she said.

'What do you say, Lisa? Shouldn't this ritual be included in a Hindu wedding as well, with a vain hope, believing that the ultimate goodness of the human heart will surface in that emotion inducing moment, and that it may very well be the last available, protective barrier to a matrimony that is forced, and thrust upon by parents for whatever reasons?

'Reflecting on the incident that you just mentioned, it is entirely possible that an otherwise sane and a sensible individual can succumb to the enormous and incessant mental and emotional pressure unleashed by the parents in matters of matrimony. The person may end up giving a half-hearted nod to their parents' choice of a bride or bridegroom, out of helplessness in a weak moment. In such instances, wouldn't this rite open the door for a last minute rescue?' he asked.

'Ummmm,' she said.

Venkat continued, 'We are all emotional beings. Emotions pervade everything that we do, and emotions transcend facts, logic, reason, and objectivity. That being the power embedded in the emotions, can it be tapped into, by creating such a high decibel emotion inducing moment in a Hindu wedding?

'The perpetrators of pressure—the father or mother—won't they break down and confess they had pressured their son or daughter into the matrimony against his or her wishes? Isn't it possible that they experience a moment of transformation, and a realization of their unkind and sinful act? Or won't the boy or the girl muster the courage to clearly disclose in front of the large gathering their disinterest in the matrimony, and that may be lot more impactful than what has been relayed numerous times in private? I would imagine that's what happened with the girl whom you mentioned. Won't the very fact that there is such a ritual in a Hindu wedding, deter parents from forcing their children into such matrimony?'

'Venkat, why are you getting so philosophical and emotional on this topic?' she enquired softly in a puzzled tone.

'Lisa, my point is, this ritual should be included in a Hindu wedding as well. Maybe, it will not have any favourable bearing in a forced matrimony. But it doesn't hurt to have this included.'

After a deep pause, Venkat added, 'At least I think, it could have saved mine.'

Lisa asked with a deep sense of shock, 'Venkat, you said you were single?'

'Yes, Lisa, I am now,' he said.

My Hot Date

'Yatha Drishti, Tatha Shrusti' (The world is as you see it)

I heard this in the Vedanta study class. So, I told myself not to take my life too seriously, and instead take a lighter look at things around me.

And this is what I saw.

It's a Saturday evening. I have a headache. My headache usually occurs when I have not eaten well. I just finished breakfast, but the headache persists. I decide to have a filter coffee. I look at my brass filter coffee maker. It is a shining golden yellow, two-story cylindrical structure, with its magnificent beauty extended to about two feet in height. A proud smile crosses my lips. I had specifically requested it from India, when my sister visited me a year ago.

I open the filter lid to check for the freshness of the coffee powder inside. Like an expert, I'm able to easily discern. No! This needs fresh powder. I open the kitchen cupboard and pull out a brand new Cothas Coffee packet, and in the process, I remind myself that I should be storing the packet in the fridge, now that I have opened it, to preserve its aroma.

I walk to the kitchen sink and clean the brass filter maker by removing the old coffee powder, and rinsing it with a splash of hot water. I take a piece of cloth and gently wipe it dry.

Next, I take a scoop of the coffee powder in a teaspoon and put it into the upper level. I decide it can hold more, and put three more scoops in. It is now loaded to my satisfaction and my heart floods with joy just looking at it, and revelling at the prospect of the fruits of my labour that are soon to come.

I turn around and fill a ceramic cup with an inch of water, and microwave it for half a minute. The water is hissing with the fury of a mighty serpent. I pour the water from the cup, on to the face of the spoon and let it trickle over to the coffee powder. I repeat the process again and this time, I have added half an inch more water. Satisfied, I close the filter lid and let the powder soak in the furious water.

Inside there is a huge rumbling noise. It has become a mini battlefield. There is an intense fight between the thunder-like roaring water, and the coffee powder, which is at its desperate best to guard its virginity. It is justly protective of its virgin flavour and fights with all its strength. The water gets only more defiant at the powder's refusal to submit politely. It releases its million atoms in splashes, which devour the powder hungrily and greedily with lust. It floods the entire space and proclaims its mighty victory after a long drawn battle.

Calmed, it now seeks to explore the netherworld. It drips, drop-by-drop into the bottom level with its grand loot and rests for a long sleep ahead.

Next, I pour milk into a steel vessel, and boil it up to the point, where it rises up like a full moon in its glorious white.

I tenderly remove the top level of the coffee maker and peek into the coffee decoction[4] resting beneath. It is in a deep and quiet slumber, like a python that goes weak after a big meal. I take an inch of it in a steel tumbler and pour the milk from a great height into the tumbler, giving it a joy ride of its life. I carefully stop when the tumbler is almost full, and just a centimetre away from its brim.

Strangely, I notice life's duality unfold before me. Reminding me that both cruelty and compassion exist in life. The very raging water, which hungrily devoured the coffee powder just a while ago, is now, surprisingly, serene and composed and shares its loot with its milky soul mate with all compassion and love.

'Mmmmmmm,' I'm lost in deep thought. Life is never black or white. It is all brown; I mean grey! The water, self-

---

[4]Coffee syrup

chastened by its evil act is now an embodiment of love and is virtuous in its act of giving back.

'Every saint has a past. Every sinner has a future,' I am able to make sense of this that I heard in the Vedanta class. All of us have different streaks and they surface depending on the sum total of the environment around us. And no matter what, there is always the possibility of achieving a transformation, and evolving into a higher being, marked by purity of mind and heart.

I return my contemplation back to the steel tumbler. The coffee decoction with the milk is in joyous unison leaving foams of happiness all around on top, and beholding it is a visual ecstasy. The sensuous aroma it radiates is sweeter than a thousand roses. I slowly sip and draw the filter coffee into my mouth and with eyes closed, I take it deep, inside my throat.

I savour the moment, fully blocking my mind from everything else, but just drinking in to the moments of this blissful happiness. My mind has become pure attention. I am in the moment, and I think, I may even give a royal ignore to the divine nectar, if offered by heaven.

Just a date with coffee could be deeper moments of bliss. And as I continue to savour with my eyes closed, I ask out aloud, 'Now is this meditation?'

My cell phone rang. My trance was disturbed, and my eyes opened. I grabbed the phone to put it on silent mode, but observed it was from my dear cousin Deepika, from India.

'Hi Di,' I said.

'Hey *enna da, eppadi irruke?*'[5] she asked in Tamil.

'Deepika, can I call you back in a short while?' I quickly asked.

I was in no mood to be interrupted in the savouring of my coffee. I had barely started drinking, and wanted moments of solitude to indulge in the rest, before returning my mind to the worldly things, or even talking to my dear cousin.

'Why? Why can't you talk to me now?'

That was typical Deepika. I closed my eyes, as I took another long sip, feeling and relishing every drop of it as it went down my throat.

'I can't, now, because I'm on a hot date,' I said, smiling.

'Oh, you are outside with someone?'

'No, I'm at home,' I said absent-mindedly.

No sooner did I finish saying this, she shrieked in horror, 'Whatttttt! You have a girl in your apartment? Too much da. You have changed a lot after going to the US.'

'It's not what you think. But let me call you back and explain this,' I said impatiently.

I returned my glance to the coffee, imploring it not to go cold on me. I promised it, I will end this call, and will submit my attention to it completely, soon.

'My foot! Who is this girl? A white babe? How come you are even managing to talk to me on the phone? Where is she now?'

'Deepikaaaaaaa let me call you back. I will explain

---

[5]How are you?

everything,' I pleaded, taking another sip of the coffee.

'Just tell me her name, I will let you go. Tell me faaaaaaast da. My head will break if you don't. Is she next to you?'

I'm very fond of Deepika. I could not bring myself to hang up on her, although that thought crossed my mind.

She was stubborn and insistent when she wanted something. I was not going to have my way with her now. I was better off telling her now, and ending the call quickly, as opposed to being subjected to her litany of questions, and extending the torment.

'Hey! Ok, ok...I will tell you. However, promise me you won't swear at me, when I finish telling you?'

'Ok DA. I won't. Now don't piss me off further by dragging. Tell me quick. What's her name? When and where did you meet her? Have you had sex with her?'

My irritation at her, translated to laughter now. I said, 'Deepika, wait! Hold your horses! I'm having a hot date with hot, hot filter coffee.'

'Whatttttttttttttttttttttttttttttttttttt? You are not making any sense. Are you drunk?'

'Drunk, I am. Drunk with bliss! Ok, don't yell at me.'

And I told her everything.

'Stupid. Idiot. Assss! Ok, go and enjoy your hot steamy date,' she said and hung up.

I laughed again. She was the only one, who was capable of swearing at me like that. And she was the only one I allowed to do so.

I returned to drinking my coffee with complete attention.

This time, I turned off my cell phone. You don't want to be disturbed in your meditation, or when you are with a hot, hot date. This is a private time of bliss!

Tears in the Bathroom

It was 19 July, and Deepika's birthday. Deepika is my cousin. I had just returned from a late night dinner with friends, and it was past midnight, 12:30 a.m., while in India it was 1 p.m.

I dialled her number. It kept ringing and there was no response. I called her again after ten minutes and there was no response, still. I called fifteen minutes later and this time I got lucky. Third time is a charm, that is not a cliché, I told myself.

'Hello.'

'Hey Deepika, many many happy returns of the day. Happy birthday.'

'Thank you, da! What took you so long to wish me? It is close to 1:30 in the afternoon here.'

'Hey, I should be asking you. What took you so long to

pick up my call? Where were you? I have been trying your number for the last half-hour.'

'Sorry da. I was in the bathroom.'

'Hellooo! You were taking a shower so late in the day on your birthday?'

'No da. I wasn't taking a shower.'

'What were you doing then?'

'I was crying inside the bathroom.'

'Why? Are you ok? Is it about Kiran? Did he say or do something?'

Kiran is her hubby.

'Nooooooo. It has nothing to do with Kiran. He is always sweet to me.'

'Ok then, why were you crying?' I asked, my curiosity aroused.

'See, once in a while, I go to the bathroom, lock myself, and cry. I cry to my heart's content. It makes me feel nice.'

I was very amused to hear that, but I didn't have the energy to probe further, as it was late by my time. I simply said, 'Ok, I'm glad I got to reach you now. Sorry, I had dinner with friends at the downtown area and got back home late and hence this late call.'

'What? Partying with babes?'

'*Ella di*![6] I wish.'

'Why not? Haven't you met anyone interesting there yet?'

'I should have found my girl in India. Here, any

---

[6]No yaar! in Tamil.

interesting Indian girl I bump into, is already taken. She is either already married or has a boyfriend. It is very frustrating!'

'Look out for the American babes!'

'Well, what can I say? It is much more common to come across a good-looking girl among Indians, than among Americans. That's been my experience so far. Maybe that is why I miss India so much! In my office, there aren't any young and pretty girls. Majority of them are older, and the few younger ones are not good looking.'

'How is your search at shaadi.com going?'

'It's a slow process, talking to a few of them, but no one is really interesting.'

'Ok, keep me posted about your girl hunting. Call me again sometime next week. Go, get some sleep now.'

'Ok, bye Deepika. Take care.'

'Good night, da!'

Deepika knew I had my profile at shaadi.com, and constantly asked me the question about my girl search, every time I called her. It was very annoying because I didn't have much to tell.

I had my best friends, Mahesh and Krithika, who lived in the same city.

Mahesh and I worked for the same company, HSBC Finance. I had met them at a party, hosted by our marketing leader, Naveen Mathew. It was a small business unit, and he had invited all the Indians working there, with their families for an Indian get-together. It was my first month in the office, and I had met only a few of the co-workers before, while a majority of them who were at the party were unfamiliar faces.

Naveen is from Kerala and his wife, although a Hispanic, had cooked a lot of authentic south Indian delicacies. It was amazing to note her interest and passion, and the fact that she cooked the Indian dishes so well. I was fascinated, looking at one of the delicacies, and exclaimed loud in joy, 'Wow! There is vathakozhumbu[7] here!'

The last time I had tasted it was back in India, and it was several months ago.

As soon as I uttered 'vathakozhumbu', Krithika walked towards me, and asked if I spoke Tamil.

I said yes, and her face lit with joy. She mentioned that Mahesh and she were from Chennai. They had moved to San Diego from Virginia two years ago, but had no Tamil friends to talk to or converse with in Tamil. She was very delighted to hear a Tamil voice, and said that she rushed in amidst the crowd to meet me. That is how I had got introduced to them, and since then, they had become my best friends.

They were very kind-hearted; they called me to their house very often for lunch or dinner, and sometimes, we followed it up playing card games. We even went out together for a movie or visiting the world-famous Wild Life Animal Park and the San Diego Zoo.

---

[7]Traditional south Indian delicacy made with tamarind and turkey berry (also known as solanum torvuml).

For a single guy, it is a great feeling to be invited by a married couple to hang out with. I felt much loved. My theory was that usually married people made friends only with other married people here. Single guys were not glamorous or interesting to hang out with. But here I was lucky.

Over time, I had become extremely comfortable with them, sharing my personal things. Whenever we met, we talked a lot and had great discussions. The conversations centred primarily around two topics. One was about work place politics, and the other about the many women I was interacting with, at shaadi.com, at different points of time. And we talked about philosophy too. So when I was at their home, I had great food, great company, and great discussions! Our conversations typically went past midnight. The only bummer was that neither of them drank, but that was ok.

They took an active interest in the progress I was making in finding my life partner. They counselled me constantly, providing encouragement, offering a fresh perspective, and being my cheerleaders, asking me not to feel discouraged and stay the course in continuing the girl search.

I have been a lucky bastard. That is what my sister said once. At critical junctures in my life, I have been greatly blessed to have such wonderful people around me, who have poured love upon me like a sister, brother or a mother.

On one of my visits, when we were talking, Krithika mentioned an instance when she had locked herself in the bathroom to have space for herself and cry.

She told me that Mahesh knew it; the purpose of her

being in the bathroom. I listened quietly to what she said with amused interest.

Shiela and Anand were another couple I was friends with. I used to meet with them once in a long while and occasionally, on weekends, we went hiking together. On one of our hiking trips, I learnt Shiela was a voracious reader, and was surprised to know she had not read Erich Segal's *Man, Woman and Child*. When I met them the next time, a month later, I remembered to pick up the book from my bookshelf and give it to her.

Many months later, I called Shiela and told her I was getting married the following month in India, to a girl named Shilpa, who is from Bangalore. Shiela was aware that I had been on a girl search for a long time, and expectedly was very surprised and happy to hear the news.

She immediately queried, 'So did you ask Shilpa if she sheds tears in the bathroom?'

I was startled. 'Shielaaaa, what did you just say?'

'Hahahaha! Do you remember you lent me *Man, Woman and Child* a few months ago?'

'Yes, I do...but how is that connected to this?' I asked, puzzled.

'There was a handwritten paper tucked inside the pages of the book, titled 'Tears in the Bathroom'. I recognized your handwriting. I agree with what you had written completely. I guess you can count me in.'

I was completely taken aback. I started to jog my memory to reconstruct the sequence of events. After realizing what had happened, I laughed along with her, and said, 'No. I didn't really ask. Although that was my very first piece of writing that I had shared with her, after we had become close.'

'Very well written! For women, you can blame it on the hormones! It's a way of bidding goodbye to things that we have to accept and move on. But see, the acceptance is harder for us, again due to women's sensitive nature—again blame it on the hormones, so things we can't change, we try to accept, but with an outburst of emotions that transform us to tears.'

'Thanks Shiela! I'm still a little dazed to know how you got to read this!'

'Sorry, I started to read a few lines, but couldn't stop myself from reading it completely. I meant to e-mail you on this, but never got down to doing so. You know, Anand's parents were here for three months, and we were very busy taking them sightseeing to the major attractions around the country. Then we bought a house. Moving was not easy, and it has been very hectic settling down.'

'No worries! It is interesting to know that you read it, and remembered to ask me this question now! The whole sequence of events is hilarious,' I said with a laugh.

'Wish you the very best! Anand is not home yet, he will be delighted to hear about this good news.'

'Thanks Shiela! Bye and I will call him later then.'

I recalled I had written this on a paper in a random moment of inspiration, and subsequently blogged it. But I had left the paper in the pages of the book that was lying around my bed.

I went back to my blog page to read again what I had written.

Tears in the Bathroom

It must have been two years ago. I was talking to my cousin in Bangalore. She is married and she is quite happy and contented with life. She told me that once in a long while, she goes to the bathroom, locks herself, and cries. She cries to her heart's content. It makes her feel nice. I was amused initially, but listened quietly to what she said.

Two days ago, my best friends, K and M, had invited me for dinner. They are happily married. They are married for eight years. Moreover, K is cute too. She will say some cute things to M, in front of me! We have had countless, late night discussions about life, work, relationship and philosophy.

This time around, in a matter of describing something, she mentioned an instance, where she had locked herself in the bathroom to have space for herself and cry. Her husband knew it, the purpose of her being in the bathroom. I listened quietly again, with amused interest.

I wonder if it is much more common than I think. Tears in the bathroom!

What astonishing diversity women characterize! They have diamonds as their best friends and they have a plain, non-flashy bathroom as their best space.

I know not, for sure, why they shed those silent tears, but know this much that there must be some deeper meanings attached. Perhaps, it is their way of balancing things, coping with life's events, or perhaps, they could be even shedding occasional tears of joy, or maybe tears of pain, or it is their way of de-stressing, or even, this is their meditation.

I bet, by doing this, they are able to move on, get over, accept things, and when they step out of the bathroom, they are all smiles on their face, a cheer in their spirits. No sulking, no show of despair, no carry of baggage, no whining. They have bid good-bye to all these in those silent tearful moments and have come out recharged and energized.

Isn't this a sign of nobility? Of strength of spirit? Sign of greatness that they invoke their power within them and cope with life's adversities? Sign of mental grit in refusing to be cowed down? Sign of strength of endurance?

Sign of character? By coping with life's endless complexities in their own simple way; and moving on with hope and sunshine.

Next time around, when I meet my girl, perhaps this will be the clincher!

I would toss in an innocuous question, 'O' fair lady; do you ever lock yourself inside the bathroom and take a while to step out?' When I hear a yes, I would give a deep smile of satisfaction and know she is the one! (Hehehe).

Tears in the bathroom—It's a sign of character, I tell you!

I smiled as I finished reading the last line. On a lighter note, I had mentioned in my write up that I would pose this trick question in assessing the character of my girl. Instead,

I ended up earning brownie points, and maybe the write up was perceived as a sign of my character!

Because I didn't tell Shiela, what Shilpa had said upon reading it.

Shilpa had said, 'You are simply great. I'm proud that you are mine. I'm proud you can understand what a woman is all about. This is giving me more confidence that we will have a wonderful life ahead...'

(It is true that Deepika and Krithika shared with me that they cry in the bathroom. It did inspire me to blog 'Tears in the Bathroom'. Shiela did ask me that question, but it was after a few years of my marriage, when she stumbled upon my write up in her mail box that I had shared with her earlier, pre-marriage. Shilpa did write back those exact words after reading my write up, but she has completely forgotten about it now!)

Bride Wanted

Rarely do we use this forum for such a purpose. But this is a noble purpose.

Boy is a US Citizen, living in San Francisco. He has a wheatish complexion, good looks, and a heart-warming smile. He is from Tamil/Telugu speaking family, cannot speak any Indian language, but can understand a little bit of Telugu.

His interests are watching TV and reading books. He is an outdoor person. He is very active and quite easy going. He is very independent in his thoughts, but looks up to his parents for many things.

Looking for a girl (beautiful girl is a bonus), who is very caring, very patient, and affectionate, and who has a natural love for children.

Little flexible on height. Again, parents are keen on a girl who is a personification of patience, and loves children. So little flexible on age too.

Bio-data/Horoscope/Picture provided upon request and interest.

Please scroll below to contact the parents.

>>>

>>>

>>>

>>>

>>>

>>> Father—Sriman Narayanan, srimanpj@gmail.com

>>> Mother—Mrs Sriman Narayanan

PS:

Boy is a beauty, but very naughty. (He is aged two years and two months).

So we decided we might as well get him married, so as to outsource our headache to his wife, who can take care of him.

Hahaha.

Yes, the 'Boy' is my son Siddharth, who is two years and two months old.

I sent the above email to all my family members in our Google group on a Sunday morning, with the sole objective of evoking some fun and laughter!

I was worried if my e-mail would get lost in their inboxes,

or may not receive urgent attention and be read as I wanted. To arouse interest and ensure prompt reading, I displayed prominently on the subject line—'Bride Wanted'.

And such a title assures immediate attention, as this is a matter that is of great interest and curiosity to everyone, regardless of their age or marital status—cousins, uncles, aunts and grandparents.

As they read each line, their minds were working at a furious pace, jogging their memory on the long list of their friends, acquaintances, families for an eligible bride. At the same time, they were puzzled by the quirky description of the 'boy' and the extra emphasis on the expectation for the bride to possess an innate love for children, while saying height and age were of no consequence.

It was interesting to hear from everyone separately, later, on how they fell hook, line and sinker for the matrimonial ad of the 'eligible boy', not to mention the increased interest it attracted, considering the bridegroom was also a US Citizen, and what went through their minds, while reading each line of it.

My sister started to wonder, when she was halfway reading through it, as to why I was going public with the boy's details, without first giving a preference to my wife's parents, and relaying the information exclusively to them. After all, they had two daughters—Meena and Madhavi—and were frantically looking for a suitable boy for Meena, the elder of the two.

Meena, too, read my email when she was at work.

Beaming, she took a printout of it, came home, and told her mother (my mother-in-law, that is!) that she had received a US-based boy's matrimonial details and was very interested in his profile. Her mother could not believe her ears, as Meena had all along been adamant about not wanting to get married. Greatly excited to see Meena's interest and her change of heart and mind to consider this boy, she asked Meena to read aloud the boy's description.

Hardly had Meena read the first few lines, when her mother was nodding her head in deep appreciation and expressing her immediate approval, completely ignoring the quirky description of the boy, while being intrigued as to why nothing was said about the boy's job or salary.

Finally, she was taken aback in the end, and burst out laughing that the boy was her little naughty grandson.

My uncle and aunt said, 'Good Lord! We had a hearty laugh. Good idea and I'm sure many like you would like to follow your lead.'

I felt very pleased at all the reaction that was pouring in, and I told myself, 'Isn't it a great pleasure, and a feeling of intense joy to bring a smile and laughter on the faces of people around you!'

I'm sure, if my two-year-old son has the same sense of humour as me when he grows up, he will relish this one too, when I recount it to him.

Just as I finished that train of proud thought at my own sense of humour, and being successful at it, my phone rang. It was my mother.

I said, 'Hello Amma!'

'Sriman, I don't approve of what you have written,' she said.

'Why Amma? It was written in pure jest, on a light note! I didn't mean it, of course.'

'Please don't say or write such a thing henceforth. I felt deeply hurt. Siddharth is a little God. At your age, your dad and I were managing two kids, remember. We never complained in this manner. Kids are a bundle of joy. Spend time with them. Play with them. Enjoy their presence.'

'Sorry, Amma, I feel ashamed at what I wrote now. I didn't mean it though.'

I was on the speaker on my phone handset. My wife heard the whole conversation. As the call ended, she came towards me with a worried look.

I looked at her, and said, 'I made a mistake. I got carried away…

'When I sent that email titled "Bride Wanted"', I said smiling, 'I should have deleted my mother from the distribution list!'

(This is a true story; the title created a flurry of excitement, with no one in my family group even remotely anticipating who the boy was!)

The Greatest Conspiracy, with Qualifiers

The curtains opened.

A bright beam of light flashed on the little boy, who sprinted towards the door, panting heavily and knocked hard when he reached.

The door opened and the boy asked, 'Is it true?'

The Lord smiled and asked, 'What is it my child?'

'Lord, I heard about the greatest conspiracy in this universe,' said the boy.

'What have you heard, my child?' asked the Lord, with a smile.

'When you really want something, the entire universe conspires in helping you to achieve it, so said my sister, reading from Paulo Coelho's book,' said the boy.

He continued, 'I have been flooded with mixed feelings ever since I heard this. I have seen this being true in my own little world of experiences, in a converse way.'

'I have had an instance where I had desired something completely life changing, but not really wholeheartedly, as I was fearful that it would actually happen. And it didn't happen, by a whisker. That it did not happen by just a whisker, I could not attribute to anything but to the fact that I did not desire it with my fullest heart. Lord, please bless me into the deeper meanings. Is it indeed true that when you really want something, the entire universe conspires in helping you to achieve it? My head is brimming with many questions. One, I'm sure it cannot be just any desire; the desire has to be a righteous one for the universe to conspire in helping to achieve it. Two, one has to be worthy and deserving enough of the desire. But desires are dreams, and dreams by nature know no bounds, so how are we to know the difference between plain greed and noble dreams when we start to nurture them?'

The Lord continued to smile, as he read the boy's mind, 'So what is the third question, you have in mind, dear child?'

'And surely, O'Lord, You want the desires to be pursued with compassion, love, nobleness, and perseverance, and not with obsession or with a violent fury born out of frustration or with stubbornness. The desires have to have a righteous emotion attached, the end goals, and the means have to be nobler. Tell me, Lord, your divine statements are always loaded with a deeper underlying meaning; it is implied with suggestive qualifiers, and so are these the qualifiers to this greatest conspiracy of yours?'

'My dear child, I will say this for now. You are on the right path of enquiry. Continue with your self-enquiry, when you really want something, all the universe conspires in helping you to achieve the answers you are looking for,' said the Lord, with a deep smile and disappeared, amidst a changeover of lights and a loud booming sound, quickly followed by switching off of the lights.

There was complete silence. The stage became pitch dark. Sanjay Jha walked in, amidst a slow background score, and spoke softly. The audience could not see him yet, only his voice was heard, 'My thoughts and sentiments are similar to the little child. These spiritual messages are loaded and suggestive; they are to be fully understood by going deeper into their realms.

'Like for instance, it is said that you have to have positive thinking and hope for the best, but that does not grant an excuse for inaction or take away the responsibility of exercising due diligence or the need for putting in your very best effort.

'Yes, hope is good, but is it "True Hope" or "False Hope"? It was aptly said by someone, "True hope is based on reality, whereas false hope thrives on sheer romanticism". Or "false hope" is like jumping off the cliff with the hope that God will save you, which is being plain foolhardy. Alas, in deep ignorance, the distinction between true hope and false hope is blurred and one may act on false hope, but I suppose the spiritual law makes no allowances for the acts of ignorance. Just as the law of nature makes no allowance of the ignorance of a little child poking its fingers into an electric power outlet.

'Yes, when you really want something, the entire universe conspires in helping you to achieve it. But this greatest conspiracy too comes with the qualifiers!'

The lights were turned on, accompanied by a loud booming sound. The audience could now see Sanjay Jha, who was dressed in an elegant blue suit.

He continued to speak.

'Ladies and Gentlemen, please give a big round of applause for the volunteers of Payir, who have put up this fantastic show for you this evening. We have more than fifty active volunteers, and this is a complete in-house production, from makeup to sound effects, lighting and stage design.'

There was big thunderous applause.

'Ladies and Gentlemen, Payir was founded in January 2005, with a mandate to empower rural India to transform itself into a socially stimulating, self-reliant and growth oriented community.

'The basic belief that every human being deserves a good quality of life is the purpose of the Rural Empowerment Facilitation center. Quality of life is, of course, relative. For an Indian village, good quality of life means unhindered access to primary health care, primary and middle level education, a sustained income that meets every day needs, and a satisfactory family, social and spiritual life.

'I urge the audience to open their hearts and wallets, so that a non-profit organization like Payir can concentrate on their actual work, instead of the gruelling search for funds.

'We are very grateful for every bit of donation you are able to make today. Our volunteers will come around, and you can please sign your pledge forms and the amount of donation.

'Thank you very much for your support. For more information on Payir, please visit www.payir.org.'

There was another round of applause.

It was followed by the board of directors of Payir, presenting the details of various projects and initiatives undertaken by them, with a request for financial support and volunteering from the public.

This was the second fund raising event that Sanjay was managing for Payir in six months. It was his idea to script a small play to provide some entertainment, and engage the audience into attending the fundraiser. This was a first time, and an experiment.

He was very pleased that the play was well received. There were many in the audience who knew Sanjay personally. They came over and congratulated him for directing it, and greatly appreciated the spiritual uplifting message associated with it.

A young woman walked over to him with a pad and pen. She said, 'Sir, I'm Raveena, a staff reporter from *The Chennai Times* and am covering this event. I want to ask you a few questions. May I?'

'Sure,' said Sanjay.

Raveena pulled out a tiny voice recorder, and held it close to Sanjay's mouth, and asked, 'Sir, this play had a fantastic performance. Great spiritual message! What made you choose the theme and the message—The Greatest Conspiracy?'

'Pursuing a righteous desire with a positive attitude and a righteous emotion, against all odds, and giving in your very best does the magic, with the entire universe conspiring to helping you achieve it. I have experienced this in my own life. And I think this is what we, in Payir, believe as well.'

She asked a few more questions and noted down his email id, and phone number.

Two weeks later, Sanjay received an email.

'Hello Sir, I'm Raveena from *The Chennai Times*. I hope you remember me. I covered your fundraiser event. Attached is a scaned copy of the article on the event that was published the following day, I thought you would like to see it.

'I was wondering if you would have some time and if I could meet you over coffee?'

Sanjay replied that he could meet her the following Friday evening, at the nearby juice shop.

Sanjay walked up. Raveena was already there waiting for him.

She stood up and greeted, 'Thank you Sir, for making time for me.'

Sanjay ordered a fresh fruit juice. He said, 'So, how are you Raveena? Where do you live in the city?'

'Sir, I'm good. Actually, I'm not so good. That is why I

wanted to meet you.'

He looked at her in surprise.

'Sir, I'm very messed up in my mind, and want your counsel. I just felt a good aura and positive vibe the other day, when I interviewed you. There was something about you, and the way you spoke that made me feel very calm. So I have taken the liberty to ask you for this meeting. Hope you don't mind?'

'Tell me Raveena, what is bothering you and how can I help?'

'Sir, I have known this guy for several months, and we know each other well. Last month, I expressed my love for him and said that I wanted to marry him. He has not reciprocated, and says he does not have that kind of feeling for me. I'm so very devastated. Lately, he has stopped even talking to me, but since then, every day, I send him at least more than thirty text messages, couple of emails and numerous missed calls, professing my love for him.

'You said that when you desire something very strongly, the entire universe will conspire to make it happen. I don't see such signs, Sir.'

'Raveena, I don't purport to be any saint. But this is what I would say. You cannot pursue your love with a violence, ruthlessness, vengeance, or frustration. In those, there is no righteous emotion. The greatest conspiracy works only with a righteous attitude and emotion attached.

'If you are convinced you have given more than your best in professing your love then just let it be. Stop chasing him like this. If he is yours, no one can take him away from you. If he is not yours, then nothing you do will make him yours.

'Remember, righteous desire, righteous emotion associated with it, and giving in your very best is the key. Surely, the universe will conspire in your favour.

'Spirituality is suggestive, and, like life, is never black and white. And so also remember, when you don't see the outcome you desire even after your 100 per cent efforts, then understand that the universe has a better and grander plan for you, and is conspiring to deliver that to you.'

A tear trickled down Raveena's cheek. 'Sir, I have done a management programme after Bachelor's in journalism. In the MBA class, they taught Production Management, Information Support Management, Financial Management, and Marketing Management. But they didn't teach Life Management.'

Sanjay smiled and nodded his head. 'There are many great spiritual organizations here. If you aren't already associated with any of them, check out Art of Living. They teach you the art of living, life management.'

'Thank you very much Sir. Thank you for hearing me out, and your words of wisdom.'

Three months later, Raveena wrote to Sanjay, 'Sir, I followed your advice. I stopped my violent chase. Yet, I never heard back from Raj. But I have been actively involved with Art of Living in these three months, and have become a volunteer there. I'm experiencing a newfound joy, happiness and bliss ever since. And I believe this is the grander plan that the universe has conspired to provide me. Thank you very much Sir, for initiating me on this spiritual path.

'I want to spread my joy to all my friends and family and pay it forward.'

Sanjay wrote back,

Dear Raveena,

Happy to hear. Go spread your joy to others. Be highly devoted to the spiritual path you have taken, but never be fanatical about your own, and disrespectful of other spiritual paths. Remember, it is the righteous emotion again!

God loves diversity. Don't you see he has created thousands of flora and fauna? There are diverse spiritual paths to reach him. You stick to what works for you, but be very respectful of other paths too.

Bless you, my child.

Love

Sanjay

Sanjay Jha,

Art of Living—Kodambakkam Center,

Senior Teacher,

Chennai—600024.

The Tree and Its Secret

Kishore worked in Chennai with TCS. He travelled extensively within the south, and this was his first trip to Mumbai after seven years. When his trip was scheduled, he had connected with Priya on Facebook, as she and Shruti lived in Mumbai. They were his classmates in twelfth grade in school, and he was going to meet them after nine years.

It was a Monday afternoon. Kishore took a Jet Airways flight. On reaching Mumbai, he hired a taxi and placed his single piece of carry-on luggage into the trunk. He got into the rear seat and dialled Shruti's number.

'Hello.'

'Hey Shruti! This is Kishore.'

'Hey Kishoreee! Was expecting your call! When did you arrive? How are you?'

'Abhi...Abhi, I'm proceeding to my hotel room. I will check in, freshen up, and then come over to your place. How is Sridhar? You know the last time I saw you and Priya was at your wedding. I'm so excited to see you all, after nine years! Lots to talk and catch up on. So what time is Priya coming?'

'Looking forward to it, Kishore! Priya said she will come from her office directly; she would be here by sevenish.'

'Ok perfect! I will plan to be there at the same time. I never asked, do you have kids?'

'No kids. See you at seven then. But if you want to come sooner that would be fine too, because I'm working from home today. Give me a call, in case you get lost. My apartment is visible right off the New Link road as you come, you won't miss it. I'm on the tenth floor and I had texted you my address yesterday.'

'Great! Yeah, I have it. See you in the evening, Shruti.'

Shruti's apartment was in Malad West, a western suburb of the city. She had provided a landmark that her apartment society, Raheja Palm Spring, was behind Croma.

It was easy to locate. The society had tall buildings, fifteen stories high and he saw them from a distance. The cab driver drove inside, and dropped him near the visitor's parking. Kishore thanked the driver, and handed him the fare.

He walked towards Shruti's apartment building. She was in R block. He looked at his watch. It was twenty minutes past seven. He took the elevator to the tenth floor. Her apartment was No. 1009. He looked at the door signs, walking along the corridor, and found her apartment unit.

He could hear Shruti and Priya's loud voices from inside. He rang the doorbell.

Shruti opened the door.

'Hey Kishore! There you are! We were just talking about you. Great to see you. Come on in!' she said, and gave him a hug.

'Wow, seeing you both after so many years. You both look the same. Pretty and beautiful as always!'

'Kishore, you look different,' Priya said, giving him a hug.

'In a good or bad way?'

'In a good way, of course.'

'What will you have, Kishore—coffee or tea?' Shruti asked.

'I will have tea. Where is Sridhar? Is he on his way from work? How far is his office from here?'

'What do you think of Mumbai traffic, Kishore?' Priya interjected.

'Terrible, but these days every city is bad. So I can't complain about Mumbai. Chennai is bad, and Bangalore is worse—it's a nightmare to drive.'

'Let me get some tea for all of us,' said Shruti, and walked into the kitchen.

'How about you, Priya? How was your commute?' Kishore asked.

'Bad. This is the third time I'm coming to Shruti's house this year. Until two months ago, my office was in Andheri, and this place was very close by. Now it has moved to Dadar East.'

'I'm glad you were able to make it today, Priya! You know, this is the first meeting in my life, where I'm meeting friends, after nine years. And we have not been in touch all along. I'm not a regular on Facebook, but was glad when you found me last month. I'm eager to hear what's been going on with your lives. So before Sridhar returns, I want to ask, as he may get bored with all our nostalgic talk, so what's been with you both all these years?'

'*Garam garam chai* ,' shouted Shruti and placed the tea cups on the centre table along with a kettle, and said, 'Kishore, I will tell you my life story, and let me begin with one of the greatest life lessons I have learnt.'

Kishore reached out for the cup, sat back on the sofa comfortably, and looked at Shruti, waiting for her to speak.

Priya took a cup, smiling, and winked at Shruti.

'Long ago, there was a village, where its people, feeling burdened by life's trials and tribulations, prayed fervently to God,' said Shruti, 'that he help them, and mitigate their sufferings. God hears their prayers, and asks all of them to assemble at the village square and tells them to bring in their biggest problem in life that they want to get rid of. On the appointed day, the entire village gathers at the square. God points to a big patch of land and tells them to throw in their problems.

'When everyone was finished doing it, he finally says, "Child, now, you have a choice to make. Out of this heap, I will let you pick any problem and carry back in lieu of the one that you brought in to get rid of." Everyone rushes in and picks up a problem. It turns out that each one of them had picked up the very same problem that they brought in with them to the village square.'

Shruti continued, 'Sridhar and I are divorced. We were married for seven years. He and I are completely different individuals, with different life values. Living with him was very traumatic for me. I tried working on our marriage, but I could not take his emotional abuse any longer. I know some of my friends with worse lives, staying in a suffocating marriage or having a messy divorce. At least, I'm out of a bad marriage, and have a better life since then. I really consider my life is not as bad as my friends going through a similar situation.'

Kishore was shocked to hear this. He hadn't had any idea of it. 'Shruti, I'm sorry to hear this,' he said.

'Don't be sorry, Kishore. I believe whatever happens, is for the very best.'

Kishore drew a long breath, and replied, 'I have a similar story to tell...'

Both Shruti and Priya raised their eyebrows in disbelief.

'...No, not about the divorce. I'm not married yet, as you know,' said Kishore, 'Millions of feet above, the cosmic force has fixated its gaze. It penetrates through the space with its microscopic vision. Down below, there is a tiny spec, smaller than a billionth portion of a neutron. The earth is a speck of mass in the cosmic space.

'It takes a tiny seed, infusing life into it and says aloud, "There shall be rain, sunshine, water and nourishment. There shall be peace and threat. There shall be freedom, and bondage; pain and joy. But remember this secret and it whispers a divine secret into the seed's soul."

'And blesses it, "Thou shall be born here, where, thou is ordained" and drops the seed into the space. The seed begins its long journey, traveling in time, through space, earth's atmosphere, piercing through clouds and finally is delivered to the chosen land."

'Months go by. It has sprouted into a tiny plant now. A mile away, it sees a better land, where there is plenty more water, abundance of sunshine, free of pests and has a loving caretaker. But, the plant chooses to be calm, serene, and unperturbed at its own relative state. It remembers the little secret whispered to it, by the spiritual lord.'

Kishore made a brief pause, to fill his cup with tea from the kettle. Shruti and Priya were attentively listening.

'Years go by. The plant is a little taller,' Kishore continued, 'It derives bliss from what is provided. But, there is a fiery wind. It forces the plant down. Then the plant remembers the secret and swings back when the wind dies. There is thunder and a huge downpour. The rain drops on the plant with a force that equals a weight of a million tonnes, bruising it, tearing its leaves, injuring its stem, and threatening to uproot it. The plant shivers in pain.

'This is no ordinary pain. Its spirit and soul is deeply hurt. Tears well up. Then, it remembers the little secret whispered to it.

'Time goes by.

'The plant has become a tree. With the passing of time, it has become stronger, widening its trunk, deepening its roots into concrete land, into hard mud, spreading itself far and firm. It has grown in many parts and branched out all across from itself. The tiny plant has transformed into a majestic, confident looking strong tree.

'Time is bliss. Bless the time. The tree has grown in spirit, mind, and body over the passing of the faceless time.

'A small kid who is a witness to all this asks the lord.

"O Master, bless me with the same secret."

'And the Lord whispers,' said Kishore in a soft voice,

'"Child, the purpose of life is to grow. No matter where you are or who you are, it is to continuously grow taking every problem as an opportunity to grow. That is the purpose of life. It is to grow."

'So Shruti, my life lesson is the same as yours. Life is not about counting our problems, but it is focusing on your blessings. Life is not about questioning why we have problems; it is about taking them in your stride and growing from it.'

Priya who sat there engrossed, listening to both Shruti and Kishore, said, 'Both of you have narrated beautiful stories. Kishore, isn't it easier said than done? When you say, take every problem in your stride as an opportunity to grow—how do you seriously practise this?'

Kishore said, smiling, 'Priya, very fair question. I didn't

say I'm able to practise it completely all the time. It is not easy. But stories like these are very inspiring. I tell this story to myself. It provides me with immense strength when I'm going through a very rough time.

'Since a year, I have been going through the most painful phase of my life. It has taken a heavy toll on my inner well-being and mental health. I have a boss who is a micro-manager, and she and I don't get along. She has been making my life a living hell, wilfully finding fault with whatever I do or don't. One thing I have learnt from this experience is how not to manage direct reports.'

Kishore added, with a laugh, 'So, that is what brings me to Mumbai. I'm here for a job interview tomorrow. It's time for me to move on.'

Shruti and Priya said in unison, 'All the very best, Kishore!'

'Kishore, if you move to Mumbai, it will be exciting! We can all meet very often,' Shruti said.

'Yeah, Kishore, you and Shruti can get together often,' Priya, said smiling with a wink.

'Kishore, did Priya tell you about her husband? Sandeep is completely hen-pecked! He is very loving, and takes such good care of her. He is the sweetest guy I have ever seen. I'm so happy for her.'

'Yeah, Kishore, you should meet Sandeep. You and he will get along very well. He is so much like you. Gentle, caring, and very sweet. I consider it a blessing that he entered my life. You know, I met him in the strangest of circumstances. Since then, I have begun to firmly believe that nothing in life that happens is an accident.'

Priya continued looking at both Shruti and Kishore, 'Like this meeting we are having. Even this is not an accident. Who knows, maybe it is the hand of the cosmic force who is getting you both to re-connect with each other.'

The hint was not lost on either Kishore or Shruti.

Kishore got the job in Mumbai, and since his office was in Malad West, he decided to live close by, in Palm Springs. Shruti found him a 1BHK. They both hung out a lot. And they both hung out with Priya.

Nine months later, Kishore and Shruti were married.

On the day of the wedding, Shruti told Kishore that she had a very special gift for him, and handed it to him.

Kishore opened the gift. It was a beautiful painting of a majestic looking tree.

'Let's hang this in our bedroom,' she said, 'The tree and its secret will continue to inspire us, as we lead a life together.'

Anger and Bitterness

At the outset of the Kurukshetra war, when the mighty armies of the Pandavas and Kauravas had assembled on the plains of the battlefield, Arjuna asked Krishna to take him to the middle of the battleground so that he could take a good look at his enemies. Krishna smiled. He took Arjuna's chariot and placed it in front of Bheeshma and Dronacharya. The all-knowing Krishna did not take Arjuna in front of Duryodhana or Karna or Shakuni who were principally regarded as the cause of the war.

The Lord knew that Arjuna had a lot of anger within him. He was raging with fury. It was a righteous anger. That was acceptable. Arjuna's anger had a justifiable cause. That was understandable. But the Lord did not approve of the bitterness in Arjuna's anger, the hatred in his anger, the sense of vengefulness in him.

He wanted Arjuna to overcome the bitter emotions embedded in his anger. So, he places the chariot in front of Bheesma and Dronacharya and provokes the change into him. Arjuna shows remorse, seeing that he has to fight his own near and dear ones, his grandsire, his Guru and the sense of bitterness in his anger evaporates, his bhava[8] changes, and finally, he even questions the use of fighting. And the Bhagavad Gita unfolds to him.

To the lord, Arjuna was now fit to carry his duty and dharma, sans the bitterness, with the righteous anger and the proper bhava or 'attitude' in that anger.

I went goose pimply when the speaker explained all this in the discourse on Vedanta. It is so true.

Many a times, the very first step in the right direction comes only when a sense of awareness has set in. Stories like this sensitize us to deeper things in life. They aim to bring a sense of awareness on the art of good conduct, values, and right living.

When we do our bit, in just having this constant awareness, perhaps the law of nature will take its course and synchronize our actions to the awareness and the next time we are angry, we will check our inner selves to see if it is accompanied by bitterness. If it is, then with the awareness gained, we make a choice, to be bitter or not.

I came home after listening to the discourse, and

---

[8]Attitude, in Sanskrit.

called my mother. I quizzed her if she knew why Lord Krishna placed the chariot in front of Bheeshma, Drona vs. Duryodhana, Karna, or Sakuni. She didn't. I explained to her with great delight. I had learnt something new that was inspiring, fascinating, and intellectually stimulating, and I had to share it with my near and dear ones.

A few weeks later, I found myself bringing this up with Nargis, Rajiv, and Maya when we were at Starbucks having coffee.

Nargis laughed when I finished, and said, 'So the charmer has started giving anger management classes or what? I loved that part about the wrong attitude of anger as if there ever is a right attitude. Jokes apart, guess what, I saw *Chak de* yesterday. There was this very interesting dialogue by this Punjab di kuddi about swallowing anger. Whenever she gets flustered and out of control, her mom gives her a bottle of water and says: "*Pee le gussa pee le...*"'

'No,' I said, 'I don't mean to be preaching here. I'm just sharing the joy of my newfound knowledge. It is so intellectually stimulating. Who would have imagined there being such a deeper meaning to the simple act of Lord Krishna placing the chariot?

'"*Pee le gussa pe lee*" sure is a way of channelling one's anger. I find even writing a means of channelling my anger at times; for that matter, most strong emotions.'

Maya asked, 'I just don't get it man. The Vedanta is sometimes confusing. How can it be possible to detach bitterness from anger, is what foxes me. The moment we are able to erase the bitterness, won't the anger itself cease to exist?'

Rajiv responded, 'This is how I understand it, Maya. For instance, it is said an act of charity is really no charity at all, when done with an attitude not of charity, but instead accompanied by pride or arrogance. Even a right action is blemished when it is accompanied by a wrong emotion. It emphasizes the bhava within, and how we do things. It is surely ok to have emotions, but the key is not to let the emotions torment us. Righteous anger is ok, but let there not be bitterness in it that consumes you.

'To speak from my own experience, my previous boss was very hard on me. I could never understand his dislike for me. He hurt my career prospects by giving me an average rating. I was very angry with him and disliked him greatly. At the same time, however, I also knew that he was truly a nice man from the way I saw him interact with others. But for whatever reason, he was being nasty to me. I was angry at him, but never felt bitter towards him.'

'I agree with you, Rajiv,' I said, 'I realized that stories like these in our scriptures are full of messages that teach us the art of right living. They impart management lessons that are very inspiring.'

'Ummmm, this is an interesting conversation; we should meet more often to discuss such things. It has put a mirror in front of me to reflect how I interact with Rajiv's mother,' said Nargis, placing her arm around Rajiv. 'Rajiv, It's getting late. Let's go...the children must be waiting for us. I haven't done any cooking at home.'

Maya and I bid them goodbye.

As they left, I told Maya, 'The joy of learning! There is an adrenaline rush. I really wish I could take a sabbatical from my work and immerse myself in reading books on philosophy and spirituality, and listening to discourses on our scriptures, all day long! I see a science in it for there is so much logic and rationale embedded when the knowledge is manifested and explained by the teacher.'

And then, I asked her, 'Is it fair, Maya?'

Maya was confused at my question and its abruptness. She asked, 'What?'

I moved closer to her, and said softly in a hushed tone, 'That the woman who is sitting in front of me is so very beautiful...and she is killing me with her gorgeous looks.'

It took her a few seconds to register what I was saying. I was already smiling.

'Hello Mr Charmer, are you trying to charm me?' she asked.

I said with a laugh, 'I promise Maya. This is a righteous action, with a good bhava in it!'

And she laughed too.

Heights of Height

It was the year a major tsunami was to occur, triggered by the 9.0 magnitude earthquake near the west coast of the Indonesian island of Sumatra, striking the Indian southern coast as well.

It was a Saturday morning in June. I got up at six, which had become my usual routine on the weekends.

No, it wasn't for playing tennis, or me pushing myself for a workout at the gym. And it wasn't yoga either that made me get up so early on the weekend. It was something far more important that I had to do and wanted to do, when energy levels are far higher in the early morning.

I took a shower, and went to the kitchen to prepare coffee. I poured the coffee into a cup and walked into the living room, and sat on the sofa. I picked my laptop, rested it on the centre table, and pulled the table closer to me. I switched the laptop on, and as windows finished booting, I clicked on the internet browser and typed, 'shaadi.com'.

Drawing a long sip from the cup, I signed into my account at shaadi.com, and began to browse the profiles of the women. Yes, this had become my regular weekend grind for the past many months. I must have browsed shaadi.com more than a hundred times during these months, much as I had not wanted to. But I had no choice; I was at its mercy. It is the last resort for any single guy looking to get married.

Finding a girl through the matrimonial sites is not easy; it is a very intense and laborious process. It requires enormous amount of patience, faith, and perseverance. It is not for the weak-hearted. It is not for those who look for quick and instant results. It tests your determination and the intensity of your desire to get married.

It gets tough, if you are a guy, and I will explain the reason later and it gets tougher if you are an average looking guy like me. I will clarify, I'm not bad looking, but I'm not a handsome hunk either. So on an average; I'm an average looking guy.

And it gets far worse, when you want to marry someone who is gorgeous and beautiful, despite your average looks. And that was my issue, which made it extremely difficult, much to my own irritation, and that of my parents and family members.

Yes, I was irritated with myself too. At times like this, I wished I didn't have average looks. Otherwise, I have had no problems with my looks. In fact, I'm quite proud of them, because I have attracted many a pretty woman in the past. That is, I grow on women, and when they get to know me over time, they have got attracted to me. But at shaadi.com, I didn't enjoy such a luxury of time. I had to make an impression in a very short order, and average looks don't help when quick and snap judgments are being made about you. I was also irritated with myself that I was so particular about marrying someone really beautiful, making the whole thing doubly difficult. But I suspect I'm not the only guy to have such a desire.

Over time, I learnt a few tricks along the way in becoming smarter and more efficient in the girl search. For here, I will call it a 'girl search'. It may sound crude, but I don't mean it to be. I just don't know any better way of calling it.

One of the insights I gleaned over time was that the profiles of women that had no pictures, actually contained the hidden gems. That is, the odds of finding someone very good looking were higher among those who didn't put their pictures in their profiles. To put it differently, good-looking women were less likely to post or share their pictures upfront. So today, my target was to filter and browse only profiles with no pictures.

After spending two hours browsing, I came across one profile titled 'Beautiful Eyes'. It sparked my curiosity. This find was not bad for a morning. I had already finished two cups of coffee to keep me going and stay energized in this mind-messing search process. At least, I had found one profile that stirred interest in me, albeit with the investment of two hours of my time.

If you are wondering what was remarkable in the profile write-up that captivated my interest, actually there was nothing in it. It just had a two-line description. That is not surprising, as it is very common. I had come to terms with it. With such frugal information, there is no way you can know anything about the person. Contrast it to mine; it had three paragraphs of description talking about my interests, values that I believed in, and what I was looking for in the girl.

So I went merely by the title. I told myself that perhaps there was a beautiful face behind the beautiful eyes. It was a big leap of hope, but I had to start somewhere.

I noticed women rarely initiate interest in a guy's profile on their own. They always need to be approached. I don't know the reason, but I guess they must be bombarded with interest from many guys, and they just focus on those men who write to them. They must not have a reason or the time to initiate interest on their own, as they already have their hands full.

Or they are cautious and plain wary of any fake profiles of men that exist out there, and hence shy away from approaching men initially on their own. Else still, it could just be a carefully cultivated strategy that they cannot be seen as making the first move in approaching a guy and therefore choose not to.

Whatever be it, it was very frustrating. I had to spend

countless hours searching through hundreds of profiles, with no luxury of sitting back and relaxing, waiting to be approached by a beautiful damsel.

So I had to initiate contact with 'Beautiful Eyes' and I did. I dropped a line to her.

Hi,

Please drop in a line at Kris@yahoo.com if my profile interests you as well.

Regards,

Kris

The other thing I had worked out was, since I already had a lengthy profile write up, being succinct in the initial contact made me look good. I was not coming across as someone who was desperate, even though I actually was. The girl had sufficient information about me to decide, while at the same time, my brief one-liner e-mail sounded sincere, and cool (not desperate).

There are milestones at every step. For a guy, the first hurdle to cross is to get lucky in receiving the girl's attention or a reply from her. There is so much of competition for men even in the matters of matrimony, and at shaadi.com. So I was under no illusion that it was going to be a cakewalk getting her attention, even though I had a mention of my MNC job, being based out of USA and a high dollar salary in my profile description. There are numerous men with a similar profile of a high paying job, senior positions and based abroad. I was one among the many.

It was just hope and prayer for me from here. I wasn't sure if I would even make it past the first milestone.

Therefore, I was very surprised to see her response two days later. She wrote a line.

Hi Kris,
How are you?
Kavitha.

I have seen some merely acknowledge my message, and initial contact by clicking on the 'Accept' icon on the profile page, but not write back. I had wondered what to make of that. Did they need another email from me, and a much longer one, for them to feel pleased to reply? It took me a long time to figure this out, that it was because some of them were not paid members. They did not have the ability to respond back via the shaadi.com site, and could only merely click on 'Accept'. Since then, I had started to share my personal email id, so at least they could write back at my email id, if they did not have a paid membership.

So, this was great, I told myself. She had gone beyond accepting my interest, and actually wrote back five words.

I replied to her the same evening.

Hi Kavitha,

Thanks for writing in. It is a challenge to write the initial few e-mails!

To tell a little about myself, for now.

I work for a financial services firm in the area of risk

management. I have been in the US (San Diego) for more than a year.

Writing, reading, English movies, philosophy, are my big interests.

So much for now, for a first mail :) And hopefully, this is a little ice-breaker.

Cheers,

Kris.

She replied the next day.

Hi Kris,

Hope you are doing well. You seem to have diverse interests from writing to philosophy ☺. What do you write about?

What are your favourite books?

Kavitha.

Thus, we started to write to each other, over the next two weeks, and our mutual interest in each other sustained. This was a second milestone, and very significant. I was starting to feel good.

She shared her email id, and we had moved out of shaadi.com and were writing to each other from our personal email addresses.

She asked me general questions about my background, family, and told me quite a lot about herself. She said her full name was Kavitha Reddy, and she worked for an IT firm, Cognizant Technologies, in Hyderabad. Her interests were playing tennis and cricket. She was a big fan of Tintin and Calvin and Hobbes comics. Her sun sign was Taurus. She had a brother, who was married and was living in New York with his wife and son. She was extremely fond of her nephew who was three-years-old. Her dad had passed away, and she lived with her mother.

She said she also wanted to mention about her dark sides. She said they were her temper, moodiness, and her extremely independent nature. She could be rude and nasty when angry, though maybe not meaning a single word that she said.

I appreciated her honesty and frankness.

And I was at my natural best, able to charm her, just being myself. I had no concern about that. I never asked her any intrusive or very personal questions. I kept my conversation light, and on general topics. I had my style. Although it was a matrimonial site, and we were conversing for the purpose of matrimony, I never engaged directly on the topic of marriage in the initial interactions. That would be very business-like, and I didn't approve of such an approach. Instead, I was looking to strike up a friendship, and build on it with general conversations to reach a point where a natural comfort level set in, before getting into deeper discussions on marriage.

The more I didn't ask about her, the more she continued to open up. She said she grew up as a tomboy and by nature was a very loving and caring person, but the bull in her would rise up anytime she was pushed around. She was strong as a tiger, and although she appeared strong on the exterior, deep inside she was a lonely woman, looking for love and care from her man. She signed all her emails as 'Kavi'.

One day, she asked me if I would like to web-chat. I told her I would love to. We set up a time for a Sunday. It was morning for me, and it was late evening for her in India. She came on yahoo messenger and for the next forty-five minutes, we chatted away furiously. She had a 'great' sense of humour, and by that, I mean she was constantly cracking up about what I said. It felt very good that she was responding to my humour with smiles and laughs; there were plenty of smiley icons and 'hahaha' whenever I said something funny.

And she had a 'good' sense of humour, and by this, I mean she had humour of her own, saying things or putting them across in a way that made me smile or chuckle. She said we clicked very well from the very word go, and she found it amazing that we shared such a wonderful chemistry that we spoke as if we had known each other for years.

I was very happy. I liked her a lot. I was seduced by her sense of humour, both the 'great' and the 'good' of it. The chemistry we had shared over the emails was alive and vibrant in the web chat. This was milestone three. There were no awkward pauses or slowdown in the pace of our chat messages. We had an engaging and a fun conversation. I was happier with her comments that she found us to have a great chemistry. Coming from a girl, it was a strong endorsement.

Our emails and yahoo chats continued. Both of us were into each other now.

I was now praying that she be really good-looking. The stakes had gotten high.

One night, I sent her three pictures of mine, and wrote, 'Hey Kavi, by now, if you were thinking how I look, here are my pictures. And I wonder if the lady would be kind enough to give a glimpse of her face and her 'beautiful-eyes'? ☺'

This was a nerve-wracking milestone to cross—milestone four. A crucial one for anyone in general, but it was more critical for me. Because half the time, I would lose interest after looking at the picture of the girl, and the other half time, the girl would lose interest in me, after looking at mine. Either way, it would be a painful outcome for both concerned.

I was very restless through the night, and did not get any sleep. I managed to sleep only for a few hours, at the crack of the dawn. When I woke up, it was 8:30 a.m. I wanted to check my inbox, to see if Kavi had replied, but I had no time.

I had to rush to work, and be in the office by nine with only thirty minutes to shower and get dressed and a twenty-minute commute to squeeze into it.

All through the day, I could not focus on work. I was very distracted. All personal email accounts were fire walled at work, and so I could check my yahoo mail only when I returned home. I just kept thinking and wondering the whole day if Kavi would have responded to my email. By now, we were writing to each other on a daily basis. She would reply if she liked my pictures. And if she didn't, that was a sure sign that she didn't like me, and the probability of it was very high. There was a 50 per cent chance of it. With my average looks, I ran that big risk all the time.

Compounding it, I was also worried, what if she looked really weird, or ugly? And her eyes were far from beautiful. I would be disappointed and heart-broken. If you think I'm being very shallow in placing so much importance on looks, I will have to remind you that I'm a guy. Looks are of huge consequence to us.

As my last meeting for the day finished at 6 p.m., I ran into the parking garage, and got into my car. I sped away, driving on the side road, and took the ramp to the freeway. The posted speed limit was 65 mph. I drove at 90 mph. After fifteen minutes, I reached the apartment complex, drove into the driveway, and parked the car at the assigned space in front of my building.

I got off, and sprinted up the stairs to my apartment on the second floor. I opened the door, grabbed my laptop, and signed into yahoo-mail.

I shuddered to think what I would see when I signed in. I was hoping against hope to see an email from Kavi. No news from her would be bad news. I was just a few seconds from knowing if I had half-crossed milestone four.

Yahoo was taking forever to sign me in. Was I imagining it, or was I just short on patience? No, I wasn't imagining. The yahoo site was stuck, and my system had frozen. I pleaded with God, why torture me like this? I shut down the system and re-booted. I brightened when the Internet Explorer icon appeared. I clicked on it, and typed www.yahoomail.com.

I typed in my username and password and clicked on the 'Sign-In' button. Folding my hands together, I and stared intensely at the screen.

And what did I see! Unbelievable, I had an email from her with an attachment! Even before I opened it, I knew this was a good sign. I heaved a big sigh of relief. I had passed the litmus test. She had liked my pictures. Otherwise, for sure, she would not have replied, not at least so soon. I had indeed half-crossed milestone four.

I opened her e-mail. She didn't mention anything about how I looked in my pictures, but simply said, 'Hey Kris, thanks for your pictures. Now you get to see what your new friend looks like ☺ How was your day?'

There were four attachments. It was an excellent sign. She must have really liked me, for her to even consider sending four pictures of herself. I opened the first one, and I was shocked.

Yes, 'shock' is the word. How else can I describe that feeling? She looked stunning and mind blowing. I kid you not; she looked like actress Manisha Koirala, with shades of Gayatri Joshi of 'Swades'. She was very fair, slim, and tall with a thin smile on her lips, dressed in a beautiful blue saree. It was four weeks and three days since I had first looked her up on shaadi.com. I could not believe that I was talking to such a beautiful woman all this time. Her second picture was a close up. The third and fourth ones were with her nephew, and she was dressed in casual jeans, but she didn't look good in them. I considered myself very lucky. I had fully crossed milestone four.

I thanked her for sending her pictures, and said she looked great.

She replied she had sent my pictures to her brother and sister-in-law and shared them with her mother. They were fine about me, knowing my profile and background and said they would be supportive of whatever her decision was.

And thus, we continued to trade emails on a daily basis, and yahoo-chat as often as we could on the weekends. We had reached the next level in our familiarity with each other. I wanted someone who was good looking, funny, lively, caring, understanding and with a good sense of humour. She wanted someone who was very caring, gentle, trustworthy, unpretentious and respected her space.

Our mutual affection grew deeper. We had both removed our profiles from shaadi.com on our own, as we were going exclusive. Soon, we had begun to romance. Various terms of endearment started to pour in from both sides in our interaction. She initiated it by calling me 'My Lord', 'Sweetie-pie' and signing off her mails as 'Your little tigress', 'Your Girl Friend Forever', 'Kavi', or 'Your love'. And I called her as 'Sweetheart', 'My Fair Maiden', and 'My Love'. We also addressed each other as 'Da' very frequently. 'Da' is a colloquial word used in the south, an affectionate way of addressing someone. For us, Da also meant darling in short.

By now, we weren't talking any serious stuff, but only exchanging love notes, and sometimes multiple times in a day. She would send lyrics of love songs, and sing them to me over email. This was milestone five, getting into the romancing part.

She worked in a late afternoon shift and stayed at office until about midnight there. So I had a few hours of overlap with her in my morning when I was at work. By now, I had spoken to my friend in the IT team, to find a way of bypassing the firewall, and thus could access my yahoo mail account.

During the morning hours, I checked my mailbox constantly, at least twice every hour during the overlap hours. Sometimes, she demanded that I send her a love note every hour, and insisted on long mails. At times, when I was unable to do so, being caught up in meetings, Kavi flooded my mailbox with multiple messages asking me where I was and if everything was all right and why I was ignoring her. Or she sent an ultimatum that she was not going to leave for home until she had a love note from me. She was very cute, and I enjoyed all the attention.

Amidst all the intense love and romance in the air, we both recognized that we were not 'really' in 'love' with one another, but shared a strong sense of attraction, and we had a great chemistry going between us. That is true. I had not fallen in love with her, nor she with me. It had been just six weeks, after all! Both of us were not youngsters; there wasn't going to be any puppy love. I was glad she felt the same, and that she was the one to voice the distinction first, made it easier. I had to merely concur. I really didn't want to commit until I met her in person. Meeting in person was very, very important for me. That would be the final milestone to cross.

One day, I wrote to her that I wanted to listen to her voice, and if I could surprise her with a phone call. She immediately provided me her cell phone number. We had become so comfortable with each other, exchanging sweet nothings that I wasn't too worried about the phone call being a first between us, and how it would go. So I wouldn't call this milestone six. It would be ok either way I told myself and didn't fret about it.

I went inside in one of the empty conference rooms in the office, and called her from my cell phone. It was midnight there in India. She wondered who could be calling her at that time, but instantly realized that it must be me. She said, 'Hello'. I was very surprised. I was expecting her voice to be very sweet. It was far from that. She sounded rough; there was no melody in her voice. I was intrigued that such a beautiful face should have a voice that wasn't endearing a bit.

We spoke for about five minutes, and her voice didn't demonstrate any of the characteristic smiles and wide grins that she laced her writings with. I felt I liked romancing her better over emails and chats than on the phone.

But thereafter, our romance extended to regular phone calls in addition to the daily quota of emails. I had got used to her rough voice.

On the phone, she would occasionally call herself my wife. She said she believed in the 80–20 Rule, and that

I should subscribe to it as well. I was amused when she explained it. She said after we got married, 80 per cent of the time, she would dominate me and have her way, and 20 per cent of time, she would let me dominate her and that was fair. I laughed and told her I admired her sense of fairness.

She wrote to me once, 'What if you change after we get married (lol)?'

I asked her, 'Oh, tell me what you think I'm now, and then I will tell you if I would change or not. ☺'

She wrote back, 'Well, I think you are honest and caring. You listen to me (at least, pretend :D). Hope things don't change the other way.'

She would regularly tease me by saying, 'Be good', asking me not to flirt with anyone else. Everything was going so great between us that she said she was tense and nervous, as things were too good to believe, and progressing so fast in just seven weeks.

Although I assured her everything was going to be just fine, a bit of her anxiety rubbed off on me. I had my own concerns. She was a very sweet, gentle, and caring person. It was fun to be around her, and I had never romanced anyone like this before. But I worried, what if she wasn't actually as beautiful or stunning as in the first two pictures, and looked more like in the third and fourth pictures, where I had found her to be very unimpressive and average looking?

So, I asked her what she thought about the possibility of us meeting in person, and told her I had planned a vacation for early next year to make a trip to India.

She said, 'Kris, when you visit me, you have to bend down on your knee and sing my favourite love song, 'O'Priyatama' in Telugu. Only then, will I say a yes.'

I said, smiling, 'Kavi, I can't sing. But I will surely bend down on my knee and propose to you.'

'It doesn't matter if you can't sing now, but you can start learning from now onwards!'

'Hahaha. You must be kidding!'

'No, dear. I'm serious.'

'Are you really serious?'

'Of course, my Lord.'

'Sweetheart, is there anything else that I need to learn before I see you?'

'Yes, you better be a good kisser,' she said amidst giggles.

I was stumped. I asked, 'Kaviiii—What did you just say? I can't believe you are capable of saying such a thing, although I'm delighted at what you just said.'

'Dear, I was just kidding. Now don't set your hopes high!'

'Ahh! Why do you say something only to take it back? Why induce so much pain, sweetheart?'

'I want to assure you that I'm not taking back my condition though.'

'That I need to sing? Or bend down on my knee?'

'Are you trying to get smart with me? It's both. And you have to sing it without a mistake!'

'Oh my goodness! I have only seen women ask the guy to propose on a bended knee. Where did the singing come from, my dear?'

'I'm special, and I'm different, darling.'

'Ok, send me the song.'

'Love you, Da! Just sent,' she said with a wide grin. She was sitting in front of her laptop.

'So my love, what are you going to sing for me?' I asked.

'Helloo, you are the one who is going to propose to me.'

'Ok, then let me go dear. I had better start practising the singing. With my zero skill and talent, I need all the time from now onwards.'

'Not so easy, Mister You can practice in your time. You can't cut it into my time with you.'

'You are a sweetheart,' I said.

After I hung up, I listened to the song she had sent, as an mp3 file.

The song 'O'Priyatama' meaning My Beloved was from the Telugu movie, *Nuvu Naaku Nachhavu* (I like you) released in 2001.

The initial lines loosely translated into English go like this. I say 'loosely' because it is difficult to replicate the same depth of emotion, intensity, and meaning in a translation.

'In that blue sky, thou are the shining heavenly star,

I waited for infinite lifetimes to reach you,

My dream today has become true, beholding your divine form,

My heart is reverberating with 100 crore tunes in the core of me,

Oh my beloved, Is this real? Your familiarity, isn't it a boon?

The heart is aching deep with pangs of pain,
First love is a sweet emotion…'

Beautiful lyrics, but I decided it was beyond me to sing them, and instead I would recite a few lines of poetry for her.

I woke up the next morning, and I saw an email from her with another mp3 attachment. I began to wonder if she was now expecting me to sing another song. I opened the attachment and played it. It was her voice. She was crooning a love song for me. It was an English song; I forget what it is now. As she ended, she said, 'That was my first singing for you, Da, from your girlfriend for forever.'

I was touched.

It was week eight. I had a call past midnight. I was woken up from my deep sleep. It was Kavi. That was unusual.

'Kavi, are you all right?' I asked.

'Da, sorry to wake you up. What is your height?'

'I'm 5'7", why do you ask?'

'Just asked.'

'That's what I had put in my shaadi profile. Why, do you recall seeing anything different there?' I asked.

'No, do you know my height?'

'I think you are 5'7" too.'

'Are you exactly 5'7", or are you little more?'

'I don't know, for sure. I can check,' I said.

'I was discussing about you with my friend. And she asked me about your height. It was then that it occurred to me. Check your height tomorrow, and tell me. And tell me please, you are taller. You know, I wear heels, and I'm exactly 5'7"'.

I felt a strange churning in the pit of my stomach. I said, 'Ok Kavi. I will check and call you tomorrow.'

'Ok, good night, dear.'

'Good night, baby.'

I got up in the morning, and the first thing I did was look up my driver's license in my wallet. It had the height information as 5'7". Yeah, I'm 5'7", but I quickly recalled that I had provided that piece of information at the time of filling up the application form to apply for the California State license at the DMV office. My height being 5'7" was vividly stuck in my mind, as I remembered seeing it in the bio-data drawn up by my parents to seek matrimonial alliances a few years ago. It was 5'7" that was mentioned there. I looked for the briefcase that had a copy of it. I snatched it open, looked for a pale yellow torn file, and found my bio-data in it. I heaved a sigh of relief. Yes, it was 5'7" that was indicated there.

But I wasn't sure, if 5'7" was a rounded number or if I was exactly 5'7". I was never into sports, and so there wasn't any reason for me to check my height on a regular basis. I didn't remember when the last time I had checked mine was, or the basis of the input into my bio-data. I was working in Delhi when my parents had drawn it up, and they must have made an informed guess. My dad had said he was 5'4" and I was taller than him, and my mother must have marked me at 5'7". And that was the number I went by, when applying for the driver's license, or in my profile write up at shaadi.com.

As easy as it may sound, but being a single guy, living in an apartment all by myself, it was tough to get my height measured.

I picked up a thick book and a pencil. I stood erect, with my back against the wall, and placed the book on top of my head which was touching the wall. Holding the book steady with my left hand, without letting it slide, I bent my head down to move away, and turned towards the wall.

I took the pencil from the other hand and made a thin mark on the wall. I took a measuring tape, and tried to measure from the pencil mark to the bottom of the floor holding the two ends.

It was a struggle, and I had to do the measurement in two instalments, going as far as my right hand could reach below, while holding the tip of the tape with my left hand at the pencil mark. Made a smaller mark, and continued the measurement from that point to the bottom of the floor.

It came to 167.5 cm. I did the translation, and that was 5'6". Maybe, I had not measured right. I went about measuring the length again from the pencil mark to the floor. The reading was 167.5 cm. I didn't panic. Maybe, I had not held the book at the top of my head, erect. I repeated the whole process and made another pencil mark on the wall. But this time, the second mark was slightly lower than the first one. It meant I was shorter than 167.5 cm. I did it for the third time, and it was slightly higher than the first one. I got frustrated with the whole process and the variability in the markings each time. I gave up, and got ready to go to work.

When I returned from work in the evening, I drove around looking for a fitness centre in the nearby area. My apartment complex has a fitness centre, but it did not have a height and weight measurement scale.

I found a small gym, called Fitness for Life, a few miles from my office. I went inside and told the woman at the register that I wanted to consider becoming a member and had come in to enquire about the membership details. After she explained, I casually asked her if I could quickly get my height measured.

She looked at me and said, 'Sorry, we have only a weight measuring scale here.' I was irritated. How could a gym not have one? I left, deeply annoyed.

It was 6:30. I had made plans to play tennis with my friend, Hari, at 7:30. I went home for a quick change over of clothes, and drove towards the tennis court, which was midway from where Hari and I lived. We played for an hour, and as we started to leave, I asked Hari how tall he was.

He said he was 5'7". I was thrilled to hear it, as I was clearly taller than him that I could see standing close to him, shoulder to shoulder. I asked him if he was sure if he was that tall.

He replied confidently, 'Of course, I'm 5'7". Why are you even asking?'

I told him I was trying to get a sense of my own height in relation to his.

Hari said, 'Kris, I can see you are slightly taller than

me. You should be at least 5'8" or 5'9".

I was very happy to hear it. I asked him if he would measure my height for me. He was amused at my request. I merely told him, that I needed to put up my profile on shaadi.com. I didn't tell him anything more.

He smiled at me, and asked how we were going to measure. I pulled out the thick book and a pencil from my tennis bag. We looked around for a suitable wall that we could use. He measured my height as 166 cm. That was little over 5'5". And Kavi was 170 cm, 5'7". I was shaken.

I asked him if he would mind repeating it two more times. And each time, it came to 166 cm. This was unbelievable. I felt a huge thunderbolt had hit my head. I felt dizzy with panic and anxiety. I politely thanked him and left. I'm not sure if Hari even realized that meant he was not 5'7" but shorter than 5'5". Maybe he realized it, but how did it matter for him. He was happily married with one kid.

Somehow, I managed to drive back home. I had to call up Kavi and tell her everything. Would she even believe me, or would she think I was a fraudster stalking women at shaadi.com with false facts?

I felt deeply apologetic as I relayed the things to her. How could I have not known my height, how could I have been callous about it? This was an unexpected shock for her, as much as it was for me.

I wasn't sure how she would react. I feared she would yell and scream at me, and at my stupidity. She was calm and composed, however, as she heard me out, but very disappointed and upset. The paradise of our dreams crumbled. I was heartbroken.

She asked me if I really was sure about my height several times, as we spoke. I said I could possibly go to a larger fitness centre, and have my height professionally measured, but I had no hope it was going to come any different. I told her that I felt a 4-cm difference between us was ok, and may not be really noticeable. She said she was devastated and felt it would look very odd.

After many seconds of silence, she said, 'Let's see how the height difference plays out, when we meet in person.' I was grateful that she didn't call it the end of the chapter, and was willing to give our relationship a chance, and wait until the in-person meeting.

I felt miserable. I understood this was a very big deal for her. Personally, I thought I could live with it, how did that matter. She was attractive, beautiful, fun loving, and very caring. What more did I need? I could live with that 4 cm difference. I was worried the daily emails from her or the phone calls between us would slow down until we met in person, and I had my doubts whether she was really still keen to meet.

As I suspected, her mails were sparse for the next few days, and I couldn't bring myself to call her during that time for I felt ashamed of myself. She had all the right to be disappointed with me, and even pissed.

Until now, Kavi was marking the completion of each week since our first interaction as an anniversary, and was sending e-cards and virtual flowers since our fifth-week anniversary when we had begun to romance. As week eight passed, it ended quietly. There was no celebration, no e-cards, or flowers from her.

Five days later, she called me. That was her first call, as we had not spoken on phone since the day I told her about my actual height. She sounded cheerful, and said that we should enjoy this period of our courtship, and take things as they come when we meet, and for now, I was her sweetheart and she was my girlfriend. She also said that the clincher would be our in-person meeting, and that she was hoping and praying that a thousand bells rang and lightning struck when she met me.

That would be milestone six and the final one to cross, I told myself. But, I was very elated to hear from her. She didn't turn away. She was deeply committed to our relationship, and wanted to give it a chance. We were back to our romance, with similar intensity. She didn't hold back, nor did I.

Meanwhile, I discovered a bizarre thing that in general, men seemed to think they were much taller than they actually were. That was my new conclusion, for I began to check with many of my friends especially those who were shorter than me, and each said their height was in excess of 5' 5". I shared this with Kavi, who listened to it, but said nothing.

At the corner of my mind, I was still worried about the height difference. Blogging was very big then. I too was blogging quite actively under an assumed identity. I wrote a blog on this topic without giving any personal details of mine, but essentially conveying the whole height episode, and asking for readers' thoughts on what it was for two people to be married, with the guy being a tad shorter.

I ended my blog with the following questions.

'What do you all think? Should they both overlook the height difference of 4 cm? Would it look extremely odd when they get married? Do you have any stories where the girl is a tad taller than the guy and it has still been a happy marriage? What else would be undesirable in a match like that?'

I received three comments and all were from women.

One mentioned she believed that all that mattered was the love of the hearts, and things like height should not stop the two from the union. Another gave an example of someone in her own family circle being married with a guy shorter, and yet they made a great couple and looked cute. Third mentioned that height is a very attractive physical trait, and it is only natural that a tall woman will expect a very tall man, but in matters of heart, height or age or anything should not come in the way. It is about the union of two hearts in love, and a 4-cm difference should not come in the way.

I was vastly encouraged by their comments, and felt very good. I attached great importance to the fact that the comments all came from women. Who can better understand a woman's mind than a woman? Their comments resonated with my own experience—I was reminded of a girl, who was aspiring to be an airhostess and was taller than me, whom I had met at Toastmasters Club in Bangalore years ago. She had shown interest in getting married to me, but I wasn't ready for marriage then.

Kavi didn't bring up the topic of height later, true to her word. On the tenth week anniversary, I sent her flowers. She was so excited and happy that she showered me with plenty of kisses on the phone. She had kisses for me on emails and chats before, but these were her first kisses on the phone. She said I was the first man to give her flowers, and she was ecstatic that I remembered our tenth anniversary.

I was in a celebratory mood. After I finished talking to her, I pulled out an expensive bottle of Silver Oak, Cabernet Sauvignon, Napa Valley. I poured a glass and raised a toast for myself. It was our tenth anniversary, and things between us were going well even after that brief hiccup. She was so sweet and cute, that she just melted with my flowers and remembering of our anniversary. She was adorable, I thought.

Continuing to savour my thoughts of all that had happened between us in the last ten weeks, I poured another glass. When good things are happening, you can make the memories sweeter by revelling in them again, and again.

I called up Kavi again, and told her I was fully drunk, for I had been doubling up to drink for her too. She asked me not to drink too much, and gave me a long goodnight kiss. I had never known her so joyful; I was being showered with kisses, unasked for.

I had stayed awake late that night, and had barely slept when I got a call at two in the morning. It was my sister.

I asked her what had happened. She said my grandfather had passed away. He was seventy-five years. I was very close to him. I had to go. I told her I would call her back by ten in the morning, and hopefully I would have figured out my travel plans to confirm by then.

I went back to sleep. In the morning, I called up my boss and left him a voice message that I had a family emergency. I would be away for two weeks. I managed to get a ticket for the same night from Los Angeles Airport. Hari volunteered to drive me to LAX airport from San Diego, which was a 120-mile drive, and at least a two hour commute with easy traffic. I was very grateful to him.

I had a long list of things to attend to, and take care of, with this short notice—pack clothes, withdraw cash from ATM for the trip, make arrangements for the rent to be paid, while I was away as it was due next week. I had to give away all the vegetables and fruit inside my fridge to a friend, who lived in the same apartment complex.

I was very busy all through the morning, talking to the travel agent, and running various errands and chores. So I had no time to call Kavi. I just sent her a short e-mail informing her about my grandfather's demise, and that I was taking a flight to India the same evening. I told her I would plan to visit her in Hyderabad, before my return and I will be in touch with her soon.

Hari came on time, and I was ready with my luggage. He drove me to LAX airport. I thanked him profusely. I flew Cathay Pacific. It had a stopover at Hong Kong, before reaching Chennai.

My grandfather lived in a small town, Vellore, that is about 135 km from Chennai. I hired a taxi from the Chennai airport, to proceed to Vellore. My mother and sister had already reached Vellore by train the previous day. Ever since the time my dad had passed away, my mother was living with my sister, who was working at Chennai.

After the cremation, various rituals were performed the following three days. We attended them, and returned to Chennai on the fourth day.

Late in the night, after everyone had retired to bed, I walked stealthily to the living room, and took my sister's laptop to check if Kavi had written anything back or sent me any offline messages on yahoo. I had no contact with her for the last five days.

As expected, there was an email from her, and a long one. She wrote,

Hi Love...

Missed you a lot...Waited for you online on Sunday evening...Real disappointment :(

That's ok...can understand. I'm really sad to know about your grandfather.

Love, you take your own time...I can understand if it's not possible for us to speak for some time...Will miss you a lot, dear...but first things first...you take care of everything... We'll keep in touch through mail.

Da...I need to tell you this. I miss you a lot...lot more

than I can say. But I'm also very apprehensive about how things would be when we meet...after all this...what if things are not the same when we meet...this is eating away my head...I know you will be worried when I speak like this, but can't help it sweetie...I don't really want anything to go wrong. Probably that is why it worries me so much.

You take care and spend as much time as possible with mom. Don't worry…I'm always with u love...Miss you.

Waiting for your mail,

Your lady

I replied:

Love,

Thank you for being so understanding, and excusing your Lord for not being able to write or call you all these days. It is about 1 a.m. now; I will call you later in the day, but just wanted to tell you this now—

I missed you so much honey,
Want to hold you tight,
And hug you hard...
And kiss my little baby's face...
Again and Again...
Again and Again....
And again and again...
Love
Kris

There was a steady stream of visitors at my sister's house, mostly friends, family members and relatives to enquire from my mother about my grandfather's demise, and there were a few, who wanted to meet up with me and say hello. Amidst all the hustle and bustle, I managed to call Kavi in the afternoon. She was out, waiting for her company cab to get to the office. She enquired about my grandfather's death, and the details of the ceremony and how my mother was feeling.

I told her I had not imagined I would be making a trip to India this soon, as I had gone to the US just last year. I mentioned to her that I was looking to take a flight to Hyderabad to meet her for a day.

She was silent for a moment, and said the lightning had to strike her when she met me, and a thousand bells had to ring in her heart.

She said, 'Seriously, I miss you a lot and I'm looking forward to meet you as soon as possible. Also, it makes me a little apprehensive, because our meeting would decide the fate for us.'

I wondered what she meant by that now.

She resumed, 'Sweetheart, my cab has come. I'm getting into it and I can't talk very comfortably in front of others. Please call me later, Da. Love you.'

I borrowed my sister's cell phone whenever I could, to make brief calls to Kavi. The phone reception wasn't great, but it was better than going to the STD/ISD public phone booth to make calls, waiting in queue and having to keep the calls very short with a line of people waiting outside.

We didn't have the same frequency of daily emails because I didn't have the privacy or easy access to a laptop.

I booked my flight ticket for the following Sunday morning, returning the same evening to Chennai. Three days before I was scheduled to fly, I was browsing in my sister's home.

Suddenly, a message popped up on my yahoo messenger. It was Kavi. She was in invisible mode.

Kavi: Missed you Da.

Kris: Heyyyy.

Kris: Me tooo.

Kris: So I booked my ticket…

Kavi: I got ur mail :D

Kris: How was your day? Do you have office tomorrow?

After about a thirty-second pause, she wrote back...

Kavi: Yep, I do.

Several seconds later, she continued.

Kavi: Just relaxed the whole day.

As she wasn't typing back instantly, I got worried.

Kris: Kya hua?

Kavi: Kuch nahi :D.

Kris: Are u talking to someone else?

Kavi: No.

Kavi: Y?

Kris: You aren't replying to me immediately...

Kavi: I did?

Kris: No...u didn't!

Kris: Love, be good!

Kavi: Yes I did.

Kavi: Didn't u get my messages?

Kavi: I'm good.

Kris: Hmm. Ok Da sh...

Kavi: :(

Kris: Ur messages are crisp as well...!

Kavi: Mmm.

Kavi: Sweetie.

Kavi: Now my brother is online.

Kavi: He's asking me something that's y.

Kris: Okay Da love...

Kavi: Give me a sec.

Kris: Da, I wanted to ask u something.

Kavi: Yes sweetie.

Kavi: Ask Da...

Kris: When I come in to Hyd, if I bring in a small bag, is there a place where I can keep it and pick it up just before leaving?

Kavi: Hmmm...Not sure.

Kavi: Will see if I can get my sister's car.

Kavi: Let me see if possible.

Kavi: Else, we'll carry it around.

Kris: Hey no no...that's ok...you don't have to get a car just for this.

Kris: Just asked...

Kris: Then I wouldn't carry anything...

Kavi: No Da.

Kavi: We'll see.

Kris: I didn't know that my dear lady drives too...

Kavi: ☺

Kavi: Yes I do.

Kavi: I do a lot of things, which my lord doesn't know ;)

Kris: Hmm :)

Kavi: :))

Kris: Like what my dear?

Kavi: You'll get to know that in due course of time :)

Kris: Why wouldn't u tell me now love?

Kavi: Too many things.

Kris: U can say a few for now dear...

Kavi: Whistling in the theatres.

Kavi: :))

Kris: Oh god! I can't whistle even if I wanted to...

Kris: And?

Kavi: Hahaha

Kavi: Well.

Kavi: I told u. U would be shocked ;)

Kris: Go ahead...Tell me more...

Kavi: That's enough.

Kavi: Else, we won't have anything for us to talk later.

Kris: Hehehe...Okay tell me one more though for now...

Kavi: Can't remember.

Kavi: Lots of things.

Kavi: Climb trees.

Kavi: Ride bikes.

Kavi: Climb walls.

Kris: Oh oh...!

Kavi::D.

Kris: You are so cute. Lots of Kisses ☺

Kavi: :)

Kris: As far as the kisses go, that would be given in the movie theater.

Kavi: What?

Kris: Will your lord get a chance to hug his little tigress?

Kavi: :-O

Kavi: Very funny.

Kavi: Did I ever mention that I attended karate classes?

Kris: Hahahaha.

Kavi: I'm serious.

Kavi: And did I tell u that I intended to join kickboxing?

Kris: :)

Kris: No u didn't.

Kris: And it is too late now...

Kavi: Now u do...

Kavi: Hmm...

Kris: Would be wearing glasses?

Kavi: Who, you, or me?

Kris: You...

Kavi: I can't see without my glasses.

Kris: Just asking though…

Kavi: Hmmm...

Kavi: Would u?

Kavi: U better get them.

Kavi: It's pretty warm here.

Kavi: Carry ur sun glasses.

Kris: Okay Da...

Kris: Will talk to u tomm...

Kris: Eyes are drowsy...

Kavi: Hey.

Kris: Tell me.

Kavi: Did u forget anything...

Kavi: :)

Kris: What?

Kavi: U should know it.

Kris: No...why?

Kris: Are u hinting at something?

Kavi: Ok...

Kris: Tell me.

Kavi: :-o

Kris: Tell me fast shhh.

Kavi: :D a hug

Kavi: And a kiss :-*

Kavi: :((

Kavi: U forgot.

Kris:No i didn't...

Kris: I still haven't signed off...

Kavi: Yes u did.

Kris: A big warm hug.

Kris: And lots of kisses to my ladylove...and a good night kiss.

Kavi: U don't give me anymore warm hugs.

Kavi: :((

Kris: Reserving some of them for later this Sunday!

Kavi: Very funny.

Kris: And one more good night kiss dear...

Kavi: Ok.

Kris: Lots of hugs and kisses.

Kris: Miss you sooo muchhhh.

Kavi: Liar.

Kavi: Ok.

Kavi: Da...U take care.

Kavi: Miss u a lot.

Kavi: Be good.

Kris: Sure Da...me too...

Kavi: Miss me a lil.

Kris: Sure dear...

Kavi: Be good.

Kris: :)

Kris: I will.

Kris: Byeeeee for now...

Kavi: Bye.

Kavi: Sweetie.

Kavi: :)

My flight was at 9 a.m. I prayed to God after taking a shower. I always prayed for very important events. Whether we were destined to be together was going to be known today. It depended upon the chemistry we brought together in person, and the lightning and thousand bells she wanted to see and hear.

The flight landed in time at 10.10 a.m. I deplaned and

walked towards the airport exit door. She called me and said she was almost there, and would be reaching in ten minutes. I told her not to rush and drive safe. I walked out of the airport exit door and waited outside at the curb.

She called me again and said she had parked her car a few blocks away from the main exit door, and asked me to proceed walking straight along the line of the building towards the parking lot, and that I should see her car. It was a white Maruti 800 and she was standing next to it.

I continued walking, and from a small distance, I saw a white Maruti. When I got closer, Kavi waved her hand. And I waved back.

She was standing there smiling, in a radiant light blue suit. My jaw dropped. I am truly at a loss for words to describe how she looked. She was many times more beautiful and attractive than I had found her to be in the pictures. She looked very sexy. She had the most charming smile I had ever seen, which made her wildly attractive. Even in my wildest dreams, I had not imagined she was this gorgeous.

'Hi Kavi. You wanted to see the lightning and so here I'm dressed in white,' I said, smiling, as I had worn a white shirt. Those were my first words. She gave a shy smile. My heart melted looking at her captivating smile.

I was completely smitten. I had initially told her that I wanted to see her in a saree, and she said she wouldn't be comfortable dressed in it for a first meeting. I thanked her now in my mind, as I could not have handled any further amplification of her attractive, sexy looks.

I got into the car. She said she would drive me to the Husain Sagar Lake, which was her favourite spot in Hyderabad.

She asked, 'So how was the flight?'

'It was good, a short flight. The breakfast was great.'

I was quiet for a while, as I was still trying to come to terms with the fact that I have been romancing such a gorgeous beauty all these weeks, without really being fully aware of it.

Finally, I asked, 'Kavi, you are looking so beautiful. Seriously, you should have been in modelling.'

'My uncle is a film director. He has asked me many times to act in movies. I have told him I'm not interested. I don't like the film world,' she replied matter of factly.

The drive to the lake was more than 30 km, and it took us little over an hour to get there.

The lake connects the twin cities of Hyderabad and Secunderabad. There is a famous statue of Lord Buddha installed at the centre of the lake. She said the statute was chiselled out of a white granite rock, weighting 450 tons and was installed in 1992. It took 200 workers and two years to complete the sculpture. She also added that it was about 72 feet tall. I really didn't want to hear anything about 'height' today, and that statistic didn't impress me. But I enjoyed the whole scenery of the lake, sans the tall Buddha statute.

From there, we proceeded to have lunch at a restaurant. When we were seated inside, she said her mother wanted to say hello to me, and rang her mother from her phone. I spoke to her for a couple of minutes. We had discussed earlier that neither of us wanted this to be a very formal meeting, and didn't want me to visit her mother on this trip. This was to be a casual meeting, and we were clear that we needed all the private time for ourselves, for we just had a day.

By the time I finished talking to her mother, she had ordered bottled water for me, and handed it over to me with a smile. She told me it was very important for me not to fall sick, and she was making sure I didn't drink anything but bottled water. We chatted—I mean, she spoke a lot and I listened. I ate light. After we finished lunch, she asked me if I liked the place. I told her it was an excellent pick, and the food was delicious.

Our plan was to go for a movie next, and later hang out at a coffee shop before heading back to the airport.

We went to watch a Hindi movie, *Fida*, being screened at the Cineplex inside the shopping mall. We were a little late; the movie had started. We found our way in the dark hall to our seats. When we were seated, I tried to hold her hand; she smiled and took it away. After about twenty minutes, we didn't find the movie to be interesting, and decided we might as well use the time to talk with one another instead of staring at the screen. I had never left a movie mid-way, and it was the first time.

As we walked around the shopping mall, she said, 'Kris, although I'm happily chatting with you, you don't know how nervous I feel that I'm with you. I can feel my heart beating faster.'

That was a good sign, I thought. 'Kavi, be cool. You are doing great,' I said, smiling, 'Yes, I don't see any sign of nervousness in you, even after you tell me. Please relax.'

I seized that moment, and held her arm lightly, signalling her to stop walking. I inched my shoulder closer to her and said, 'See Kavi, I'm as tall as you are.'

I was wearing shoes that gave me the extra centimetres, while she wore flat sandals. She looked at me with a smile, and said I wasn't taller.

From there, we drove to a coffee shop.

I was having a wonderful time with her. Of course, I did not kiss her. Nor did we talk in the same romantic manner as we did in our emails, chats or over the phone. The comfort level or the ease to indulge in romantic speak doesn't automatically extend to in-person, instantly or in the very first meeting. It requires time to recreate it, and to get into that flow, and surely warrants a couple of more meetings.

We were at the coffee shop for about three hours, talking. That is, she doing the talking, and me listening to her. She glanced at her watch, and said we needed to leave to get to the airport in time. We stepped out of the coffee shop. Her car was parked on the road in front of the shop.

'Kavi, I want to hug you,' I said before getting into the car.

'You can't do it here, Da. Everyone is watching us.'

It was a busy road, there were lot of vehicles plying, and men, women, children walking on the pavement.

'Ok, Da. Where do I do it then?'

'I don't know. Maybe next time.'

'Kavi, how do you expect me to survive for the next meeting, if I don't get one now?'

She smiled. I went closer, gave her a quick hug, and kissed her cheek.

I couldn't believe I mustered the courage to hug and kiss her, however brief it was. I didn't give her much time to respond or react. I just went with the flow. I was in the moment. Having a gorgeous beauty beside me, who was chatting merrily non-stop and wearing a killer smile, it was difficult to resist.

'Everyone has been looking at us,' she said.

'That is why,' I said, 'the kiss was small, and the hug was brief.'

She smiled again. I told her I had a small gift for her, and reaching for my bag in the car, gave her a Tommy Hilfiger perfume.

We headed back to the airport. She drove fast as we were running late. She was worried that I was going to miss my flight. I really didn't want to leave her.

'I have been talking non-stop all day with you,' she said. 'I have never spoken so much in my life in a day, Da.'

We reached the airport, managing through the busy traffic just in time. She brought the car to a halt, and before getting off from the car, I kissed her again real quick and told her, 'Kavi, I will miss you.'

She said, 'You have been kissing me all day.'

'Hellooo, that was just my second kiss for the day,' I said, smiling, 'next time, I can't promise I will be this frugal.'

She looked at me, and said, 'Very funny,' and continued, 'You need to run Da. You have only thirty minutes for your boarding call. The security check gate must be on to your right when you turn back. I will call you in a few minutes as I exit the airport terminal. Miss you, sweetheart.'

I looked at my watch. I barely had much time to get to the boarding gate. I had to run.

I said, 'I will miss you too, Kavi. Drive safe, and call me.'

I turned back, entered the airport lounge, and walked towards the security check gate. The line was long, but it was moving fast.

As I cleared security, she called me and said, 'Da, I'm already missing you so much. Take care, sweetie.'

We spoke for a few minutes, and we were back to our romancing on the phone.

'Kavi, too bad! Why didn't you let me hold your hand?' I asked.

'Da, why didn't you persist,' she replied.

'Did I have to persist?'

'Yes, the way you were hugging and kissing me.'

'You know Da. Someone so very beautiful like you, it was very ungentlemanly of me to have had kissed you only twice. Next time, I will make up for it,' I said with a laugh.

'Very funny. Ok, Da, be good. Don't flirt with the flight attendants. Text me once you land. Miss me.'

'Hey, listen.'

'What?'

'Da, you have a brilliant charming smile. Mine pales in

comparison with you. From now on, when my admirers say I have a dil-se smile, I will tell them that there is someone who has got a better smile.'

'You are complimenting me too much.'

'I mean it Kavi. It was such an unexpected thing. Wonder how you were hiding that smile from me for the past twelve weeks!'

'Well, I have been carrying the same smile for twenty-six years! Shouldn't you be running to your boarding gate now, it is already late dear?'

'Ok, love, if you insist that I really need to leave. You drive safe back home.'

'Miss me, sweetheart. Have a safe flight.'

'I will, miss you.'

'Liar!'

'Hahaha. You are a sweetheart! Ok, I'm really running now to the gate.'

My heart was brimming with emotions as I walked to the boarding gate. For the first time in twelve weeks that I had known her, and for the first time today, I began to fantasize how beautiful my life would be, being married to her, and living with her. Those thoughts entered my mind as soon as I met her in the morning as that was when the whole thing became very real. But it was only now I had the privacy of time to indulge in them, to daydream.

My heart was screaming with joy, and I said, 'Life is Beautiful!'

I was choked with emotions. I took a piece of paper

and started to write. With my heart flooded with pure joy, and emotions running high, words just poured out. I had to keep pace with it, in writing it down.

I dialled her number.

'Hi da.'

'Hi Kavi, have you reached home?'

'No da, Why?'

'How long are you away from reaching home?'

'It will take me another twenty minutes. There has been heavy traffic here.'

'Ok, can you please park your car for few minutes? I have to say something right now.'

'Aren't you getting late for your flight? You must be boarding now.'

'No, I'm at the gate. My flight is delayed by forty-five minutes.'

'Wait, I'm pulling my car to the side. Ok, tell me quick.'

'Kavi, I have never written poetry until now. This is the first time. You have triggered them in my heart. You had wanted me to sing your favourite Telugu song—"O'Priyatama" for you—But here, I'm bending down on my knee, and reciting my own song that I just wrote for you—*Meri Kavitha ke liye, meri ek kavitha,*' I said in Hindi. I was all emotional. People were looking at me, as I was talking on the phone with knees bent on the floor. But I didn't care about anyone.

I spoke slowly, reading out what I had written:

Radiant white, you are,
Fair like the creamy milk,
They make me go still,
Your soft beautiful eyes.

Your cheery sensuous lips, pretty face,
Heighten your smile,
And you don't know much,
How they weaken my heart.

O' Little fairy,
Whisper this secret,
Deep in my ears,
Promise to keep it to self,
Tell me please, are you the full moon herself,
Come to grace this Earth?

In cheer, your face waxes a bright smile,
In thought, it wanes into a silent smile,
And that is why, I wonder,
O little fairy,
Are you the full moon herself?
Come to grace this Earth?

Can I come close to you, I know not.
For there is thousand watts around you,
A high voltage smile, you have,
Makes me say,

O'little fairy,
Please be with me always,
Don't go away.

She laughed, and said, 'Liar'.

I asked, 'Whattt?'

'You say I'm thousand watts, and wonder if you can come close to me. But you were hugging and kissing me all day long.'

'Why are you stuck on that?' I laughed, but slightly annoyed. 'It was just a small hug and two kisses. Don't you have anything romantic to say in return?' I asked.

'Thank you, da. That was very sweet. Email your poetry to me. It is getting late. I don't feel safe having parked my car in the middle of nowhere. I need to get going. Talk to you tomorrow.'

I boarded the flight, and my head was continuing to flood with thoughts of her. When the plane landed at Chennai, I pulled out my mobile and texted her that I had reached.

She texted back, 'Good night sweetheart. Call me tomorrow.'

I reached home, but I could not really sleep. I was tossing on the bed, with nervous excitement. My sister and mother enquired about my visit in the morning and what I thought of Kavi. I told them I liked her much and wanted to marry her. They were pleased to hear it.

I called her that evening, but could not reach her. I thought she must have been busy at work, being the first day of the week.

I emailed her on Tuesday, 'Da, I have been just thinking of you the whole day and the whole night. I didn't get sleep as well. I would admit you had never occupied my mind so much since the last thirty-six hours! I called you yesterday evening. Are you busy, sweetheart?'

On Wednesday, I checked my email, and there was no reply from her. That was very unusual. I wondered if everything was fine, and sent her a panic mail. I told her I was very worried, and asked what was wrong with her that she had neither called me back, nor emailed me in the three days since I had left Hyderabad. On Thursday, I sent her two text messages pleading that she at least reply something to assure me that she was safe. Her silence was killing me.

On Friday, I finally saw an email note from her. I had a strange feeling just looking at her email, even before opening it, because I had been expecting her to call me and not send an email.

My heart was beating hard. I opened it, to read. It was the beginning of the end.

I remember the date. It was 14 September 2004.

She wrote,

Hi Da...

How are you doing sh...?

Sure, you must be cross with me. Da...I'm sorry for all of it. Never really meant to hurt you in anyway. Seriously Da, there's a lot running in my head as of now. You've nothing to do with it, Da...You are too sweet; believe me too sweet...

Da...I'm confused about everything. Did you notice I look like a giant in front of you…? Just need some time to think clearly. I truly enjoyed the whole day with you. But Sh, that alone is not enough for making a decision. It holds the same for you too.

Sh...I'm damn lonely at heart. But da...I don't want to use you, just to have somebody by my side. It's not fair Sh. Yes, I may be hurting you now, but this would avoid all the hurt in future, for both you and me.

I, frankly, didn't get much time to think about anything since we met. I have been thinking about everything a little, but can't really think clearly. Need some time to understand how I feel.

As soon as I came back after meeting you, my mom asked if I had made any decision. And my sister asked me in the morning about it. Then my brother and you have been sending emails and text messages. To be frank, I'm not in the right frame of mind to think about anything. The whole thing is, all this takes time, and I really want to make sure things are right. It's both our lives at stake.

I'm apprehensive about everything and since Monday evening, I've not been in my normal mood. I have been thinking about everything, and can't understand anything.

I just want to take enough time to take a proper decision. I don't want to take a decision now. I will relax and think about it. Take my own time. For good or bad, I want to be sure about my feelings. I'm really very emotional and impulsive. That's why, I don't want to make a decision in a hurry and repent later. Want to be sure about it. Da... Hope you understand. We will deal with the whole issue as two adults.

Da, remember when I told you that if things don't work, we would still be good friends and still share a good relationship. I really mean that. But that doesn't mean that I'm looking to run away. Just need some time to make sure that what we really feel for each other is true. Hope you understand...Please, no hard feelings, Da.

Love

Ur lil tigress

I was shocked. It felt as if I was being crushed by a 10,000 lb force. I wondered how she, who was totally into me, could bring the whole thing to a screeching halt. It had turned out to be a roller coaster. My joy and happiness had burst like a bubble.

I wrote back to her.

Hi Kavi,

Although you suggest in this mail that you need time to decide, the fact as I gather sensing from your mail is that you have decided already.

What do I have to say? All I ask is, if you truly care for me then tell me the real reasons for whatever you have decided—no matter how hurtful you think it would be to me. And it's only in the absence of the truth, that you would be causing me hurt tremendously and I won't be able to find a sense of peace.

I know that there is something more than this that you aren't telling me dear.

Because height was a known thing from the very start and didn't become an issue on the day we met. Dear, you had made a mention a few times for sure, before we met, that you are in love.

Waiting for your mail,

Kris

She replied the next day,

Hi Kris,

I thought about the whole thing long and hard after you left on Sunday. I couldn't really make up my mind about anything until say Wednesday or Thursday. Yes, I did know about the height before we met. But dear...didn't I mention it number of times that we'll decide only after we meet and spend time with each other. Sweetheart...The fact is that lightning didn't strike.

Yes, I did feel extremely comfortable with you. I had never spoken so much in my life in a day. Did you notice I was speaking non-stop the whole day? I really like you. That is for sure. But, that alone is not enough. I've seen it in the past that just being comfortable and enjoying each other's company is not enough. There is definitely more to a marriage. Frankly speaking, from my end, unless I fall for a person madly, I don't think that I would give in even a little, no matter to whom. And I didn't really get that feeling when I met you. We share a good chemistry, but not enough to get married. And I don't really want to get into a marriage without a strong feeling. Because at the end of the day, not only will it leave me hurt, but I'll end up hurting others.

But da, the decision I've taken was only after thinking about everything. I don't want to hurt anyone. I know I've done that now, but it would be very little compared to what we could go through in future.

Dear... You have seen me. I'm very impulsive, independent, dominating and extremely restless. I react first and then think. And you are exactly the opposite of me. Dear, initially we would give in to a lot of things. But later on things will get difficult. It's not a matter of one day, week, month, or a year. It's a matter of a lifetime. Frankly speaking, until I said it yesterday, I didn't really make up my mind. It's not been easy on me either, dear. And I think this is the best for both of us.

>>>> da, you had made a mention a few times for sure before we met that you are in love.

Da, did I really commit myself on that...I've restrained myself from saying those three words since the beginning, because I didn't really want to commit myself until and unless I was sure about it.

And da...don't you think I look like a giraffe next to you...? I really prayed to God that you would be of my height if not more. And it didn't seem to work actually. Otherwise, things seemed to be fine.

Sweetheart...everything would seem ok in the beginning. But in the end...things would be different. Keeping all these things in my mind, I've taken this decision. Because a wrong decision will destroy two lives. No matter what, I don't really want either of us ending up hurt.

Hope you understand...Never meant to hurt you, nor would I ever do that intentionally...Take care Da...

Waiting for your reply,

Kavi

A tsunami of pain engulfed my heart. I felt devastated. I wondered, why God would even let me meet someone so beautiful if there was no way I could have her in my life.

I didn't know what to write back to her. I always believed in 'mutual liking', and there was no way I was going to try to persuade her. And I really didn't feel that she looked like a giant or giraffe in front of me. With my shoes on, I was at her height.

In-person meetings are always the clincher. I knew that. But here, we had known each other for twelve weeks; she had developed strong emotional feelings for me, and given this backdrop, I thought appearances would not matter for her, and she would go beyond it. I was not expecting this outcome in the least.

I didn't call her before leaving for the US, I was heartbroken.

Upon my return, I checked my emails, and she had written a couple of them.

17 Sept. 2004

Da...Come on Sweetheart...why are you ignoring me... why are you not mailing or calling me...Hey don't know if you are checking your mail, but happy and safe journey, my lord. Please mail me after you reach. Take care and be good. Miss you...

Waiting...

Your Lady

18 Sept. 2004

Da...it's 18th, exactly 00:05. Waited for your call until now. I guess you have decided not to call. Well hope/wish you have a safe and a happy journey. Hope to see mails from you after you reach the US. Don't know what actually triggered your anger or whatever you call it, you didn't call up even to say bye. Just take care and be good. Miss you a lot...

Miss you a lot...

Good Night Honey

Ur loving lady

That week, I met up with my friend Arun and his wife Ritu, who were visiting the US from India, for a drink. Seeing my depressed look, Ritu enquired if I was nursing a heartbreak. I looked at her puzzled; was it so obvious on my face? I told them the whole story.

As I finished, I lamented, 'I always thought that unlike men, once a woman falls for a guy and develops strong emotional feelings for him, then looks are of no big consequence for them. And here, she was so much into me, romancing, and emotionally very attached, I really didn't think height or physical appearance was going to matter to her to this extent, although she did mention that it was important for her beforehand.'

The words Ritu uttered are still ringing in my ears.

'Kris, every woman,' she said, 'has her own rules. Each woman is different. You have to understand that.'

Ritu's words reminded me of a conversation with Anushka when I was doing MBA; she was my batchmate. Anushka told me that she may flirt with a guy with killer looks, but she would not marry a guy who was too good looking or handsome. Such a guy, she said, would attract a lot of attention from other women. It meant running the risk of her man getting very conceited about his looks, developing an attitude and possibly becoming morally corrupt. I was plain astonished to hear that someone could very deliberately not want to marry a very handsome guy. Yes, every woman has her own rules. Each woman is different.

I did respond to Kavi's emails subsequently. I told her I was so shaken by the turn of events that I didn't get to talk to her before I left.

Kavi was sweet. She made herself available to me whenever I called her, or replied to my emails although her conversations had become briefer, and her emails shorter. I think that helped me to pass through that difficult phase. It would have been tougher had she gone silent on me completely and shut me off after the meeting. Although the warmth was missing, she did appear to look forward to my less frequent emails and calls.

I told her I was going to stop contacting her for a couple of months to get over my feelings for her. She asked me not to...that we could still be good friends and continue talking. I told her that would be possible only after I got over her, and for which I needed space and time of no contact.

Those three months passed. I just focused on my work to distract myself, and not let my mind dwell on thoughts of her. I was partly successful, but it wasn't easy.

It was 26 December, a Sunday. The television and newspapers were flooded with images of the tsunami that had hit the Indian sub-coast. I thought, my own tsunami was nothing compared to the pain, suffering and havoc caused by it.

The following Saturday morning, I woke up to the burst of fireworks in the celebration of the New Year. I closed my eyes in silent contemplation, and told myself—Today is another day. Just anything is possible. Life can be beautiful. Saying this, I put my profile back on shaadi.com.

Five more months passed. I had exchanged a handful of emails and off-line chat messages during that time with Kavi. They were very casual and brief messages.

It was a wonder, but I had moved on. Is the heart a beauty or a beast?

It is a beast, as it is such a vulnerable design of God. All it takes for it to be immobilized and start getting attached to someone is a handful of days of warmth and affection. It goes weak and aches, and longs to be with the person always. I had known Kavi for just twelve weeks, but couldn't imagine my life without her. Can there be anything more fragile on this earth than this heart?

It is a beauty; it is a beautiful creation of God. It never gets stuck or fixated on anyone, and is rarely stubborn. With time as a healer, it moves on and gets over it. The heart is able to transcend its own deep past affections and yearnings for a person, and grow out of it by reaching out to the new ray of hope, the new sunlight, and the new rainbow in front of it.

In that death-like moment, the heart sees no purpose in life without her; but fast forward in time, and the heart finds her of little consequence whatsoever in its life now. Can there be any greater miracle than this on earth?

It is a beast, but a beauty too.

I have no regrets about having met Kavi because it was a beautiful experience, although I was disappointed about the outcome then. But it taught me, heartbreaks are common. They are more common than we usually hear of, in our society, movies, or books. For we celebrate successful love stories but don't hear the countless stories of heartbreaks.

That is life. Heartbreaks are part of life. It is ok to have a heartbreak. What is truly essential is whether you are able to bounce back and move on in life. One heartbreak is not the end of life. There are other doors that open up for those who have faith and prayer.

I realized we go through various experiences in life, talking of such romances, but not every time can our finite sense of mind and intellect understand or rationalize why they had to occur if there wasn't going to be a happy outcome. It is the journey, not the destination.

Maybe surviving heartbreak should be viewed as a badge of honour. Your mind and soul is burnt and charred in fire, but with remarkable strength and endurance, you survive the battle scars, the bruises, and the wounds. That deserves a 'Green Star'.

I'm not ashamed to say that I have earned a few Green Stars in my life. At least, that is how I look at it. They make for wonderful stories to tell, like the one I told just now. And the earlier one I narrated about Rita Noel. Or the next one I have to tell, which may perhaps be a book on its own.

And I met my wife at shaadi.com. Seriously, not kidding.

(The long web chat immediately preceding Kris's visit to Hyderabad, and the subsequent exchange of emails between Kris and Kavi post their meeting, are reproduced here verbatim as they occurred).

Acknowledgements

My many thanks to my sister, Ramya Rohini. I'm blessed to have her in my life. She has been a cheerleader of my writing and that helped me believe in myself, for I value her feedback greatly. Thanks, Akka, for your loving support on this book journey.

To my cousins, Sowmya and Sharath, who seeded the thought in me to publish a collection of short stories.

The stories in the book were written over a period of ten years, based on my personal experiences and inspired by life events around me. While the title story and 'Heights of Heights' are real stories, others are primarily drawn from incidents that occurred in my life, and I have woven in a bit of fiction to turn them into stories.

I discovered the joy of writing, when I stumbled upon

blogging, and the interaction with the readers made it very therapeutic for me, when I was going through some of my very low moments in life. Thanks to my blog friends at Rediff and Sulekha, without whom I may not have continued 'writing'. I clung to them, and looked forward to their comments and views each time I posted a new writing on my blog page, and their feedback helped me to continue to believe in the style of my writing.

Thanks to Priya Sivan, my very first blog reader at Rediff, and to Ash, Resh, Venkat, Sapna, Sowmya. And Thanks to Nargis Natarajan, Sajitha Rasheed, Ekta Bhandari, Priyanka, Priyamvada, Maria S., Rithu11 aka Krithika Mahesh—I had a great time hanging out with them at Sulekha.

I'm very thankful to my wife for her total and silent support, providing me the space to write. It's funny that she has not asked to read any of my stories yet. I'm not sure, when she eventually reads some of my past experiences, that she is going to take them with a smile, even though they occurred much before I met her! And I hope her three sisters (if at all they get to read my book) do not share all that they read about me here! ☺

Thanks to everyone at Rupa. It has been great working with them.

My thanks to my mom for her blessings.